Darque
&
Obscure

Nick Kisella

Darque & Obscure
A Black Bed Sheet/Diverse Media Book
April 2015

To Kim and the twins.
Rich, here's another one.

ACKNOWLEDGMENTS

Thank you Janel Speigel, for the support.
A special thanks to Nicholas Grabowski and Black Bed
Sheet Books for helping me bring Louis to life.
Thanks to the fans for reading and enjoying Louis
Darques' adventures. There will be more to come!

FORWARD

The basement.

Bruce had remained on the chilly concrete floor since being hurled from Dantilian's pit in Hell. Scant moments had passed since his arrival, but it felt like an eternity. With each painful breath he took, all he could smell was the fowl scent of brimstone permeating the air. His tiny body, still twisted and bloody from his injuries, shuddered as he struggled in a failed attempt to stand.

Healing had begun swiftly, as he'd expected since being cursed with immortality, but there was too much excruciating pain to move voluntarily yet. As he laid there in a sticky pool of his own blood, bones knitted together, jagged wounds gradually pulled closed. All he could do was wince and gasp in

1

agony, a man that was a raven, unable to scream out his own pain, unable to have a voice. Bruce didn't know if what he used to hear with while trapped as a raven were still called ears, but whatever they were, they were ringing, and every beat of his heart throbbed through them.

'I'm a person!' A thin voice in his mind shouted, 'A man, a human being!'

A human being, he thought sadly, knowing he'd never be human again, nor would he ever die because of the new curse put upon him by the demon-man and brother to Louis, his best friend, Obscure.

Before he could think on it further, a blinding sharp pain, like a lightning bolt, struck him. His body shifted and twisted as his spine forced itself to straighten again and heal where it had been broken. The sound of his bones popping and grinding made him wince, and he craved the hands of a human again merely to clench them into fists.

The idea of being a man once and having a normal life was suddenly too far from his mind, especially while thrashing about on the cement floor of the basement in Louis' brownstone. He shook out his wings after they had sufficiently mended themselves a short time later and began picking away at the thick clots of blood on his feathers with his beak, searching the room for Louis.

The flickering of a few candles shed dim light in the expansive room. The wavering luminance made him dizzy for a moment until he was able to finally right himself on unsteady legs.

The battle in Hell, the triumph over B'lial and the price he paid, none of it mattered at the moment. Bruce just wanted to find his friend in the darkness.

The room was still and quiet, until Bruce strained and heard the muffled sobs coming from the far corner off to his left. He twisted around in the darkness and saw Louis, crumpled into a ball, on the floor with his back against the wall. The man visibly shuddered with sobs and Bruce could see tears shimmer in the dim light of the room. The raven painfully kicked off the floor, stretched out his wings as wide as he could and gently floated across the room to land haphazardly in front of Louis. He squawked and pecked lightly at Louis' bare feet to get his attention.

Louis sat back slowly, his head lightly hitting the wall behind him. His face was covered in blood and filth, streaked clean by the wetness of his own tears.

"I'm sorry, so sorry." His voice was a hoarse whisper; tear filled eyes fluttering open, glowing deep red in the darkness. "I wanted to make things right, but all I did was make things worse." He shook his head, "We're no better off now than we were before."

Bruce squawked and shook his head vigorously, ignoring the pain lingering in his tiny neck. He wondered why Louis couldn't see that even though things ended badly, B'lial was finished. The nightmare was at an end, the demon couldn't hurt anyone anymore.

The war was over.

ONE

His escape was the night sky.

Louis slipped outside to the balcony and silently pressed the French doors closed behind him. The action of lifting his head to the stars hurt. His entire body still ached, and he vividly remembered why.

Why. Reasons, so many; as many as the stars he'd managed to see before lowering his head to halt the pain.

"How can life be like this?" His words were small, gruff tones in the darkness of the night. "Everything hurts. Everything always hurts now."

Louis slipped a thin pack of wine flavored cigars out of his jacket pocket and removed one from the pack. He stared at it for a moment, lost in a mix of feelings and memories. He tore the cellophane off the cigar and crumpled it into the front pocket of his jeans while tugging free a lighter to light up.

The smoke tasted smooth and sweet. A welcome friend he shared with no one; exactly how he liked it.

Again he thought, *'Why?'*

"Why does everything have to hurt so damn much?" He whispered. "I know life isn't supposed to be easy, but-" He cut himself off and the memories drifted through his mind.

Mere days prior, partnered with Bruce, and a demonic looking twin brother he'd only recently discovered existed, Louis fought his father, the high ranking demon, B'lial, in the bowels of Hell. During the battle he was wounded so badly, hurt so deeply, that he realized even as powerful as he truly was in a physical conflict, pain was so much more than just a physical feeling. It transcended his flesh, as if his very soul, his core, had been torn asunder and writhed in agony, a grain of sand lost in the heavens, the stars.

His mind painfully rested on an image of Bruce, nearly torn in half and burned badly. Louis couldn't even imagine the suffering he had to have felt. Sure, the raven healed quickly; it was part of his curse, but still....

"He's still cursed because of me, and now it's even worse." Louis inhaled again, shaking his head. "He gave up everything for me out of loyalty. Now he's got nothing but misery. Immortality, but trapped in the form of a raven."

Slipping the pack of cigars back in his pocket, he slowly walked to the railing and reached out to grab it with both of his hands while inhaling deeply from the cigar.

Suddenly the railing was gone.

Louis could smell her perfume wafting to him on the slight breeze. The scent was unmistakable.

DIANE.

Louis felt as if his heart had abruptly stopped beating. Confused, he was suddenly surrounded by inky darkness with only his love, long thought lost, standing before him like a beacon in the night, a symbol of hope that he never dared imagine before.

Cloaked in white, a glowing brilliance surrounded her. She reached out for him with both hands, beckoning. The disease that had taken her from him had been clearly wiped away. Diane looked as beautiful, young and healthy, as the day he'd met her a cruel lifetime ago.

The tears came without him even knowing it, filling his eyes and blurring his vision, but they weren't tears of sadness. He rushed forward, gripping her in a tight embrace, his body shuddering. He wanted to scream out all the pain he'd lived through without her, how each day was a new lesson in hell. Feeling her face pressed tightly against his chest, he wanted to fold her up, encase the bright light of her inside him so he'd never feel that agony again. So he'd never know darkness, never be without her again.

Diane pulled her face away and looked up at him. Her eyes bore into his own with a warmth he'd never thought he'd feel again.

"I love you Louis, and that love is forever." Diane's words held a silent strength that she passed onto him, and he felt himself stand taller as he held her. "I'm so sorry you've had to endure everything the way you have. I wish I was with you, but you did the right thing by letting me go. It was my time. Take heart Louis, as you're not alone in your life either. There are those around you that care. You can share your life with them as well. In the end, I promise you that what we feel, what we have, will never end. No matter what happens, no matter how things are now or how they get, good or bad, the part of us that is love will be together in the end."

She smiled up at him, but when he tried to speak, she stopped him with a gentle finger over his trembling lips.

"No words." Diane said, stretching upward to kiss him.

Louis went with it, falling into her kiss, long and deep. He closed his eyes and held her as tightly as he dared, the warmth of her sweeping through him like a gentle wave.

And then she was gone.

****

Obscure's wounds had healed quickly but he felt drained after literally throwing his brother Louis and the cursed raven Bruce out of Hell. He stood tall in spite of his weakness, a testament to the new power he had; the new 'wholeness' of having a dark half to his soul.

"I am my father's son, and I am finally home!" He shouted.

The pit he stood in, Dantalian's realm, still bore the acrid scent of his father's remains. It was his pit now, and everything B'lial had dominion over was now Obscures', his right as his son.

"Do I want all this?" He rasped, puzzled. Obscure suddenly felt a sense of disorientation, and he didn't like it at all.

His new minions had already gathered and disposed of B'lial's remains. Only a few of the demons remained in the cavern. Most of them were low level creatures. Some of them were sifting through the pit of scattered trinkets and belongings in the pit at a lower level from where he stood.

"All of you!" Obscure shouted, voice booming through the chamber, "Be gone from my sight."

His voice roared like thunder in the pit, and the demons fled like frightened rabbits, leaving him to himself in the hazy cavern. Obscure's thoughts returned to when he tore the heart from his B'lial and stole the darkness away from the wretched creature that called himself 'father'.

"The shadow of my father, his darkness," Obscure thought to himself, "It was so overwhelming at first, all the anger and hatred. It was such a rush. There were so many foul emotions locked up inside him. I had no idea…." The demon rubbed his tired eyes and took a deep breath. "That stench of tainted emotions is inside me now, a part of me. Such feelings, I've never known them so strongly before." He looked up into the crimson haze and shook his head, frustrated and even more disoriented. "I don't understand what I'm feeling. Am I damned now? Perhaps I was too hasty in casting Louis and his pet away. He has knowledge of being damned as I have never known."

He remembered how the demons in the pit, his new minions, had encircled him immediately after he'd cast Louis and Bruce out of Hell. They'd snarled and grumbled at him in approval and though he was still disoriented from accepting B'lial's darkness, he threw his arms up in victory and fiercely howled back at them.

Before Obscure could think on it further, he found himself facing B'lial's minions again. There were demons of all types, sizes and shapes. Some looked somewhat human, while others, goblins and drudes, he couldn't even find words to describe. One of the larger demons stood at the head of the group.

"Surely you have no desire to remain here, in the pit of Dantalian, a creature of failure whose blood is on your brother's hands. Will you have us prepare your new home for you?" The demon asked quietly, head bowed, his thick wings tensing. "As you must know, your father's home is yours. We can bring you there and prepare his chambers for you to occupy and reside in."

"Not yet." Obscure murmured. He stared intently at the demons before him, eyes finally focusing on who he thought of as the leader of the group. "I've things to do before I christen my new home. Prepare it for me so that when I return it will be ready. I will choose a suitable replacement for the fool Dantalian at my leisure." He eyed the group. "One of you will rise in rank because of his failure."

The demons rushed off without pause. Some of them took to the air, while others faded into dark gray clouds of smoke.

"I'm already accepted here. It's never been like that anywhere before. This is what I wanted, it's been my desire since childhood, a dream I thought impossible to fulfill." Obscure muttered quietly when he was certain they had all fled. He shook his head slowly, looking around, *"I'm home."*

TWO

It was an early October morning, chilly but bright. Christian Mathers, twelve years old, walked down a quiet Manhattan street under a perfectly clear sky. He wore a black sweatshirt, black jeans and dark sneakers. In his black attire he resembled a very skinny, short priest. There was a slight skip to his step, as if he were extremely happy for some unknown reason. He looked around wide-eyed and watched the dying leaves, numerous and colorful, letting loose from the assortment of neighborhood trees to swirl in the morning breeze. The glaring sunshine made it look to him as if some of them were on fire, floating flames looking for a place to land and burn.

"I really love it when it looks like the air is on fire." He chuckled, smiling into the glare of the sun. Christian stopped and knelt down to lift up a couple of dead dried out leaves.

"Sometimes death looks so pretty, in spite of itself, so full of color, at least for a while." He muttered to himself, letting the leaves sail out of his hands with the light breeze. "Life itself is so much more unattractive, gray and pointless. I wish more people could see and understand that."

The boy stood up and continued on, staring directly at the sun. The brightness didn't cause him to squint; it only made him smirk and shake his head. He welcomed the warmth on his skin. "It's such a beautiful day." He ran his fingers through his dark hair and continued on down the street.

The church, Byzantine Catholic, was on the corner across the street from where he walked. He noticed it immediately because of its wildly ornate stonework and brightly stained glass windows.

"Byzantine, just the place I was looking for." He said quietly, nodding at his own realization. "It looks very old school, more than I expected. I bet they still don't pray in English most of the time." He said thoughtfully. "I wonder if they have any of those tiny squares of bread soaked in wine handy. I can use a snack and I really hate the wafers most churches have."

The church was indeed an old-fashioned looking stone building with enormous elaborately carved wooden doors and stained glass windows depicting various scenes from the bible, leading up to when Christ was crucified.

"The Stations of the Cross, what a cool story," He said absently. 'It's so very colorful." In the distance, the windows reminded Christian of the individual panels from a comic book, telling a larger than life story with characters in full vivid color.

The boy slowed his pace until he came to the corner then waited for the street to be clear before he crossed it. Though the acrid scent of exhaust fumes still lingered in the air, there weren't many cars on the road. The morning rush hour had just passed.

The stairs leading to the doors of the church were concrete, stained with age and chipping at the edges. He liked the way they looked, weathered and well used. He also liked the fact that he was able to climb them silently.

The sun was behind the church, so the doors were shrouded in shadows. Christian liked that. The irony of a place that brought light to many lives being veiled in darkness pleased him.

He didn't see her leaning back in the corner of the entrance until she stepped out into the light.

"Church?" The woman asked sarcastically. "You must be recruiting again." She was tall and thin, dressed in a black business suit. Her hair was as black as her clothing and much of her face was covered by the dark sunglasses she wore. "Still trying to find favor in the eyes of the Master, huh? Hoping he'll add a few years onto you again?"

Christian nodded and smirked, blushing slightly.

"I haven't seen you in a while Mother," He stopped in front of the doors.

"I told you never to call me that in public," she said with a chuckle. "It sounds so, *parental.*"

"I apologize, *Lily,*" he said with a smile. "I've missed you."

"I knew you'd be coming here, and I have some important business to attend to in the general area. I owe an old friend a favor from a long, long time ago," she inhaled loudly, nodding at him. "A woman's work is never done," she sighed. "I'm going to need the souls you acquire now, at least for a little while. Reaching your adolescent years will have to wait a while longer."

"For the 'favor'?" Christian asked,

surprised and slightly annoyed. "Such dedication, I had no idea anyone had such a hold on you."

"You'll understand in time. Ultimately it's going to help you as well as my friend. You may even find a place in Hell permanently when all is said and done." Lily nodded to him with a smirk. "In the meantime, I'll be around now and then to check up on you as I usually do. After all, you are my youngest. I always like to keep an eye on my baby."

Christian blushed again, his eyes downcast to avoid hers.

"Good, I always enjoy spending time with you Lily. We always have such fun together." The boy nodded. "This is a rather pleasant city too, full of such rich and heartfelt sin; in some ways the people here are very creative. I hope you find your own work here enjoyable as well."

"I'm sure it will be." Lily turned and walked away. "If you're going to confession again," she paused and turned back to look at him, "try not to take too long. Things always get complicated and extremely messy when you take too long." She turned and strolled away casually.

"I remember what you taught me. I'll try my best to make it quick and clean." Christian called out to her. "I promise."

"Oh, and do give my best to your *'foster*

parents'," she said. Her brow rose in a backward glance. "That is, if they're still alive."

Christian replied by shaking his head, his eyes dancing with humor.

The boy returned his attention to the church doors. He ran his hands over the carvings on them, the crosses, enjoying the feel of the smooth wood before pulling on both brass colored handles. In spite of their obvious age, the door hinges must have been well oiled because they swung open without a sound.

The scent of incense assaulted his nostrils as soon as he entered the room. He could see clouds of it floating around the room like swarms of tiny insects. It annoyed him thoroughly, and nearly caused him to sneeze. He turned to one side and saw the holy water in a bowl on a short pedestal next to the doorway. Christian laughed to himself and flicked the fingers of his left hand through it, causing steam to rise up. His skin sizzled and sounded like bacon on a skillet.

"Ouch," he said emotionlessly. "This place must actually have some true believers, but not enough to keep me out."

Christian held his smoking hand in front of his face. His eyes widened and he chuckled yet again, watching his skin; the smoldering burns, heal as he continued further on into the church.

The interior of the church was lit dimly by round tubes of glass hanging vertically from thick chains attached to the ceiling. In front of him there were countless rows of wooden pews, with a wide open aisle down the center and on each side. Christian walked down the center aisle, the skip to his step suddenly gone. He looked around and saw that there were only a couple of people seated on his right side near the front altar. They were older people, wrinkled with age, praying the rosary quietly, and as he willed it, they didn't even notice he was there.

"It's early, and not even Sunday." He muttered, continuing to walk. "They must have done something pretty nasty shit in their lives to be that guilty and paranoid about getting into Heaven."

Lining the walls were racks of small candles. Some of them burned tiny flames, their flickering adding an eerie light to the room. Christian avoided them all together in favor of the three small-adjoined rooms to his left.

The confessionals.

"If I were a fly on the wall," he thought to himself, "the wonderful sins I would have heard about."

Christian stepped into one the confessionals and quietly closed the door behind him. It was a small room, with only a dim light in the ceiling. He sat down on the hard wooden bench inside and stared at the square white screen on the wall in front of him expectantly.

He heard a panel slide open and suddenly the white screen became brighter. He could hear someone's rough breathing on the other side of the wall. There was a faint scent of wine and cheap cigars.

"Bless me Father," Christian whispered with a snide smirk, "for I have sinned. It's been a month since my last confession."

"My son-" The priest began, his voice clear, but just above a whisper.

"Please Father Benjamin before you say anything else, I need to tell you that I know. I know everything, everything that there is to know about you. My mother, my true mother, has told me everything. She makes sure I know a lot of things, especially about people like you, and even me. For instance, I know that I shouldn't exist, and the fact that I do is itself a terrible sin, but I also know what you do, and what you've done. In some ways it makes my own existence seem rather trivial, because for you to do such incredibly horrible things and be a mere human, well you've outclassed me by far." His words were calm and emotionless. "I'm here this morning to make sure your efforts have not been in vain, and you're rewarded, well rewarded in the realm of your true master. He has an insatiable need for men like you. He always has a need for the truly wicked."

Eyes bulging in shock, Father Benjamin Norse pushed himself back in his seat and twisted around in a frantic attempt to reach for the tiny door latch.

His hand never even got close.

The sound of the white screen being torn open was muffled, as was the final gurgling gasp of Father Benjamin Bradley as his throat was torn open.

"See, now that didn't take very long at all."

Christian promised to tell his mother how easily he took the priest, and how good the warmth of his sins tasted.

****

The coffee was lukewarm by the time the edge of the cup finally touched his lips, and Louis didn't even notice, he just sipped and exhaled smoke, trance-like. The image of Diane vividly remained with him all through the night, and all he could do was wonder if he'd actually seen her, or if he was fooling himself with an illusion to ease his own pain and guilt.

"I have to get out of this funk I'm in." He said, forcing himself to think about normal events and the news he had just read about in the paper. "If it was just my subconscious working overtime I have to get past it as fast as

I can."

The morning newspaper was a crumpled mess on the table in front of him.

"The world has truly gone mad." He mumbled, shoving the paper further away and wiping the ink stains off of his hands with a napkin. "Oh Christ, I don't even use words like that; *'mad'*. What in hell is happening to me? I sound like an idiot! The solitude must be getting to me!" Flustered, he angrily exhaled a cloud of smoke.

Bruce flew into the room, a cackling mass of glossy black feathers soaring through the sweet smelling cloud of smoke. He landed, roughly skidding to a halt on the newspaper and began gesturing toward the front of the brownstone with his entire upper body.

"Okay, I get the picture, someone's here." Louis stood up and smashed out his cigarette before making his way to the front door. "Is it Tindilli?" He twisted his head to ask the raven, who had abruptly perched himself comfortably on his right shoulder.

Bruce nodded silently and the door chime sounded off suddenly.

"Well, you beat him to the punch." Louis laughed. "I didn't even notice the sound of his car pulling up. I'm slipping. I've got to be more careful."

The raven nodded and screeched in agreement.

"I love the man like an extra father but I don't even want to answer the door." Louis said, shaking his head. "He has no idea what I've been through since the last time we spoke and I really don't want to have to tell him. He'll just end up feeling sorry for me and I -"

He could hear Tindilli mutter annoyed curses on the other side of the door.

"Oh Christ, I better answer it before he gets too angry." Louis nodded to Bruce, who flew off his shoulder when he opened the door.

"Louis! How nice of you to come to the door." Tindilli said sarcastically. "I was starting to wonder if you were home, or if you were even still alive." His expression grew somber and he stared at Louis. "Seriously, you had me worried buddy. Things were pretty grim the last time I saw you."

Louis' shoulders slumped and he felt guiltier than he expected.

"I'm sorry John, honestly. I just haven't really been up to seeing people lately. I haven't even left the house once since I got back." Louis replied, "I guess I really should have called or something." He stepped aside and gestured for him to come inside. "I have some fresh coffee if you want a caffeine fix. Please, come in and make yourself at home."

"Yeah, some coffee would be good right about now." Tindilli nodded then walked past him, headed for the kitchen. "You can fill me in on what happened with your father and that newfound brother of yours."

A quick abbreviated version of the events in Hell flashed through Louis' mind, and he went with it. *"He doesn't have to know how horrible my fight in Hell truly was, especially after what happened with his son. He already knows too much."*

"Well, that'll be easy enough to tell you about." Louis said, getting John a mug of coffee. "My brother and I, with Bruce, we confronted B'lial and fought him, like I told you the last time I saw you. It was tough, a bloody brutal fight, like I've never had before." He sat down across from his friend at the kitchen table and lit a cigarette. "But then again, I never imagined myself having super-strength and fighting a demon in Hell."

Bruce flew into the room and landed on the nearby countertop.

"Hi Bruce," Tindilli said to the raven with a nod. "It's nice to see that you made it through things as well."

"Yeah, but he paid a really high price for the victory," Louis thought to himself bitterly, *"all because of me."*

"You told me about the whole typewriter thing with him," Tindilli nodded to Bruce. "You're quite a typist little guy."

"As long as I can still ink the ribbon he'll have a way to talk to me." Louis smiled.

"Did you ever think of maybe getting a laptop or something that he could type on more easily?" Tindilli suggested. "I bet you can get one of those programs that would even give him a voice. It would be cool to actually hear him."

"That's food for thought," Louis replied nodding at Bruce. "What do you think? Do you want to be heard?" He asked the raven.

Bruce turned his head sideways in thought then shook his head and made a high pitched shrilling sound.

"I guess that answers that." Louis rolled his eyes. "Picky little guy aren't you?" He laughed and then turned to face Tindilli again. "I don't like using a computer much myself these days. There's just something about them I don't like anymore. Besides, when I do research I seriously doubt any of the texts I use are anywhere online."

"You're not really missing much." He smirked at Louis. "The whole 'social networking' thing is utter bullshit. It's just a way for adults to continue to act like they're in high school; same cliques, and now people believe whatever they read online, which could be anything from a three-headed bigfoot to a ghost that gets a woman pregnant."

"I honestly have no use for something like that." Louis laughed dismissively. "Sounds like more trouble than it's worth, just useless drama."

"So tell me, what happened to you and your brother?" John asked, quickly changing the subject with a nod and a sip of his coffee.

"As I was saying, we went after B'lial, and all Hell literally broke loose. Needless to say, B'lial didn't appreciate my brother and I working together against him. We both got hurt, and when I say hurt I really mean we should have both been dead several times over. Even Bruce, well, he nearly got himself cut in half. I had my doubts there for a minute during it all. I didn't give up, and in the end we succeeded." Louis took a deep drag from his cigarette, leaned back and sighed a cloud of smoke. "It took everything we had, but we beat him, John. Together we destroyed our father. It's all over. B'lial's gone."

Bruce nodded and made a shrill sound again, nodding vigorously at Tindilli.

"Yeah," Louis looked at the raven. "We beat him alright."

"What happened to Obscure? That was his name, right?" Tindilli asked. "Does he even have a 'real' name?"

"My brother? Not that I know of. He decided to stay there in Hell, taking over for B'lial. He has every right to since he's B'lial's son as much as I am. Personally, I don't want any part of Hell and if it was up to me I'd never travel there again."

"Doesn't that mean you own a piece of Hell now too?" Tindilli savored another sip of coffee.

"Technically yes, I probably have quite a chunk of super hot real estate, but my brother sort of made it clear that I'm not welcome in Hell anymore; not that he could really stop me from going there if I wanted to. I guess when you think about it, half of what my father had is mine, but I have no reason to lay claim to any of it. Besides, Obscure seems to fit right in there, and he always wanted to be a part of something, some society. From what my brother said to me, he's had a lifetime of terrible rejections and lived a horribly lonely existence. He's been pretty much a homeless person his entire life, in and out of shelters. Part of me feels genuinely bad for him, even guilty because I've had it so much better than he ever did. I don't know how he could have survived the way he has." Louis looked away from Tindilli, staring out the kitchen window wistfully. "I wonder how things would have been for both of us if we'd met when we were younger. Life would have been so different for the two of us if we were able to work together." He turned to look back at his ex-partner. "I don't think Obscure's a problem at the moment and I doubt he'd come here to cause any trouble anyway. He got what he wanted and probably really just wants some sense of normalcy and some time to heal."

"So you're safe now?" Tindilli looked at him skeptically. "And he's found his *'normalcy'* in Hell. Well isn't that just special?"

"I think so." He laughed. "Bruce and me, we came home after all was said and done needing some serious downtime to recover. It took a few days for me to heal completely, and I'm still a little sore here and there. That's really why you haven't heard from me. It was a little rough for the first day or so. I think I was in less pain after getting shot in the head."

"Does this mean you're, well, back to normal again?" Tindilli looked a bit confused. "Like a regular guy?"

"I was never normal, I just didn't know it." Louis sat up in his chair and gulped down the last of his coffee. "Destroying B'lial didn't change that. I'm still me; the product of a woman and a demon. But defeating him made me free of his evil, his desire to turn me into his lackey. Now there won't be anyone out to get me, at least as far as I know. I'm free of it all, and as far as I'm concerned there won't be any trips to Hell anymore."

"So the only thing that's different is the fact that you don't have to worry about B'lial coming after you again? You still don't age and stuff? You can still do that trick with your shadow?"

"Well, actually I can do a bit more than

that these days." He quirked up his brow and shook his head. "I kept wondering about what B'lial and Obscure could do with casting illusions, and I wanted to see if I could do it too. I had no idea how they did it so I just sort of used my will power to force it to happen."

"Did it work?" Tindilli asked, giving Louis a strange look.

"Yes and no. The first time I tried it I ended up stopping time in my study. I was reading an old Lin Carter novel about a guy that can manipulate energy."

"You mean the actress? I didn't know she wrote books."

"No, this is a guy that wrote a lot of cool science fiction and fantasy stuff. Anyway, his character could see energy in waves and bend it to his will. I tried that with the clock on the wall, and instead of becoming what I wanted it to become, time stopped in the room until I turned it back on again. It was freaky because the only thing that it didn't affect was Bruce and I. When I got a little used to it, I was able to change things up a little and create some illusions, which was really cool because I can make things look the way I want them too."

"Wow, that's amazing and kind of scary too." Tindili said. He looked down and suddenly the long tail of a mermaid had replaced his legs. "Oh my God!" he shouted, kicking out of his chair. For a split second he stood up, the large green tail holding him up where his legs should have been, and then suddenly his legs returned.

"See what I mean? Cool or what?" Louis laughed.

"Hey, don't go doing that again without warning me first," Tindilli laughed half heartedly. He pulled a cigar from the breast pocket of his jacket. "Do you mind?"

"No, go right ahead, though I didn't know you started doing that again." Louis mashed out his cigarette and slid the ashtray toward him. "Cindy must be pissed."

"She's a little upset, I can tell, but I think she's a little more laidback about little things after what happened with John Jr. We came so close to losing him, too close." Tindilli said sadly. "If it wasn't for you -"

"If it wasn't for me he wouldn't have been in the position he was in to begin with." Louis snapped. He abruptly stood up and turned away from John, the anger and guilt twisting into a knot in his belly. The sense of responsibility hit him like a punch in the face, and he couldn't help but feel horrible for what John Jr. had gone through just because he was a friend of his father's.

"How am I ever going to live with everything that's happened?" Louis thought to himself. He shook his head and grabbed his pack of cigarettes. *"An innocent kid nearly died,*

suffering in Hell forever because of me."

"Listen, I didn't come here to debate with you about my son's near death experience." He said sounding slightly annoyed. "What happened, happened for a reason, I'm just very grateful that you were able to help us. He's doing much better now."

"Then what did you come here for, besides making sure I was alive?" Louis turned and lit another cigarette.

"You need to go to church with me." Tindilli grinned.

THREE

Christian was always famished after a fresh kill. He chalked it up to the strain on his body during the transformation into his demon form. So he bought a couple of hotdogs from a street vender a block away from the church, greedily chomped them down with a cold soda, and walked home. He expected to hear sirens sometime during his walk, a sign that the priest had been found. When he didn't, he was a little surprised.

"I guess the illusion I cast was much better than I thought it would be." He said to himself.

He congratulated himself. Christian

masked his presence upon entering the church, so he knew he was safe from any suspicion since it would look as if he'd never been there to begin with. Whoever found Father Benjamin, which was merely an eventuality, he or she would be in for a big surprise. It would be a surprise that Christian was sure he'd see watching the news later in the day.

By the time he'd stepped through the threshold of the Cape Cod that served as his current residence with his foster parents it was past noon, and he felt like taking a nap.

"Hey Mom, Dad," he said pausing in the doorway, nodding casually to the slowly decomposing bodies on the living room couch. He had them situated to look as if they were sitting there relaxing and watching television. "I've had a long morning. I need a nap, but I'll be sure to come down for dinner."

The bodies of Steven and Jane Sanders were already beginning to reek. He'd slit both of their throats cleanly the previous evening with a razor while they slept and then enjoyed dining on their blood, savoring the coppery tasting liquid warmth for as long as he could.

"Drinking it always makes clean-up so much easier." He thought. "Mother taught me well." He laughed to himself remembering how sweet the sound of their hearts pumping was as their lives drained away. "And I really enjoy watching the life leave their eyes."

One of the first times that Christian had been fostered, he tore apart the older couple he lived with, and ended up with blood and guts all over the place. It made staying there after the kill, which he enjoyed doing, impossible.

The Sanders were better than most. They were young and strong, their sins fresh and invigorating to him.

"They actually wanted to adopt me too." He picked up a picture of the couple from his nightstand and smiled. "They had no idea what they were getting into. It was a pleasant seven months, never the less."

Christian knew he'd have to pack up and leave soon, abandon his identity and create a new one for himself, but for at least another day or so he'd stay there and enjoy being alone among his dead prizes. He enjoyed the solitude.

As soon as he was on the road again he'd end up getting picked up by the police or some 'concerned adult' worried over his welfare and get a fresh start. Then after a time, when he was bored, he'd kill again. It was always like that each time he was placed with new 'parents' no matter what state he was living in at the time. They always cared for him as best as they could. Some of them may have even liked him before they unwittingly learned who and what he was, but they all ended up stiff and stinking in the end.

****

Obscure.

His heart and mind were in chaos, torn between the peace and certainty of the sadness that he'd always known and the hatred and anger that had just been injected into him. Light and dark had clashed inside him and meshed together as they should have always been, but it was far from a comforting thing for Obscure.

He suddenly felt trapped. He felt pain in the blended misery and fury.

All Obscure could think while he solemnly stood in the pit was how to get away, to anxiously return to his true home: the streets of the city where he had a benign existence of survival and no desire for blood or souls. The city streets were what he knew, what he was comfortable with; his peace. Even people, normal people, and how they looked down upon him; it was something he was used to, something he could trust and knew how to deal with.

He missed it all more than he ever thought possible and he'd only been away from it for a short time.

'Obie' or 'Goliath' as he'd been called on the streets missed the few human friends he had, especially Jack, but he was dead and not destined for the fires of Hell. Obscure knew he'd never see him again because of that. He silently cursed B'lial for murdering his friend, and the others his father had torn apart, just to win over his brother Louis. Ultimately B'lial had done it all for nothing.

"Have I lived too long among humanity, become too much a part of it for life in Hell, what I've always longed for and where I always belonged, to be unappealing now." He thought, frustrated. "This doesn't make any sense!"

The longer he was in Hell the more conflicted he felt, the more he didn't know whether to laugh or cry. It was as if his own body was rejecting the very darkness that made him whole.

"I'm finally not forsaken, can't be forsaken, and yet I have less peace here than in a world where I'm shunned and looked down upon." He said gruffly, spitting on the rusty colored dirt at his feet. "What's happening to me?"

He thought back to a time when his father had visited him in a children's shelter run by nuns. It was one of the first times he'd met him and Obscure was so young his wings hadn't even grown out and his horns weren't even buds yet. The only thing that separated him from normal looking children was his skin, which had the texture of sandpaper and was patchy and gray. He even had long glossy hair back then.

Obscure had always had a difficult time

sleeping at night as a young boy, so he took to sneaking outside to walk in the courtyard of the shelter to look at the night sky. Sometimes he sat on a swing hanging from a tree at the rear of the property so he could experience the wind in his face like other children. They never wanted him around when they were on the swing. He was always sad and confused about his own existence, and why no one wanted him; why he could never find a foster home like so many of the other children he'd met. It didn't seem fair.

"Why do I have to look like this?" He'd call out to the night sky over and over again, hoping his rough gray skin would somehow magically soften into something more normal. "What did I do to deserve this?"

That night was one of the rare occasions that B'lail appeared to him as if in answer to his call. He wasn't frightening to him like the first time they'd met, but on that particular night Obscure was already upset because his roommate had found a foster home and moved out. He didn't want to be alone, and was very jealous of the other boy's good fortune. B'lial's words during that short meeting were not of caring and concern, but more like taunts about his very existence.

"Jealousy is good feeling son, embrace it," B'lial growled. "It will give you strength in ways you'd never expect."

"I just want what everyone else has." Obscure whispered. "Is that so wrong?"

"What did they name you again?" B'lial said snidely. "Your *legal* name, not what you've chosen to call yourself, and sure as hell not what I would have called you." The demon touched his temple in mock deep thought and then leered at him. "I think it was 'Daniel Smith', wasn't it? They had to come up with something, and since you were found in the trash without any parents to speak of, well, you know how it is; they had to call you something and give you a number like everyone else in this godforsaken country."

"They really think you have some sort of skin condition too." B'lial stared at his son with a smirk. "The nuns, the misguided fools and their inept doctors just cover you in salve and bandages, hoping it'll all just go away. You'd think holy people like them, the fanatics that they are, would be able to tell if something inherently evil was standing right in front of them and not someone with a terrible case of psoriasis." B'lial said to him in the courtyard that night. "Fools," he scoffed. "I'd kill them all myself if it didn't go against the Master rules right now."

"How am I evil?" The young Obscure asked, "I've done nothing to anybody."

"Evil?" B'lial let his wings open, blocking the night sky from Obscure's view. "You are, as I've told you before, my son. I am a demon, one of the fallen. You're the fruit of my loins, so you can't be anything but evil. You came into the world in sin, and I seriously doubt you'd survive getting baptized, not that anyone would try."

"I don't feel evil. From what I've been taught, everyone is born into sin." Obscure said, his voice sounding so tiny, so much like a normal young boy when faced with something impossibly upsetting.

"Well, that's your first problem right there. You can't always believe what you read, and especially what you're taught by these dried up old penguins." B'lial laughed. "You were right to name yourself 'Obscure' because that's what you are. It's a fine name. Here, even as a boy, you're an outcast, an abomination, yet you want them to take you in as one of their own. How can they when you look like such a diseased piece of meat walking around? Wait until you start growing up; then they'll see how powerful you are even with what they consider your 'handicap'. To me you look great, but you're too human inside, too soft. At my home in the pits, you could never be accepted as you are now. You don't even have within you the darkness, so you're useless to me in Hell, and this world has no place for you either. No one wants you."

B'lial's words were stunning to his son,

who could only stand there and stare at his father.

"So you're telling me I don't belong anywhere?" Obscure's heart sank even further than it already had at the sound of his father's heartlessness. He wanted to howl out his pain into the night, but could only stand there, impotent as his father went on.

"I may need you someday, which is the only reason why I've kept you alive," B'lial scoffed. "But as far as I'm concerned, right now you're no good on Earth or in Hell."

The memory struck Obscure as very telling. He wanted to let his rage fill him up that night so he could attack his father for treating him the way he did, but he knew there was one important thing he lacked at the time: hope.

"I have the darkness now." He said gruffly. "Yes it's a revolting, but it's made me whole, I can feel it, so I can do everything my father did, even Louis." Obscure's lifted his head and his eyes brightened with hope. He remembered Louis and all the advantages he had being born of demon and woman, and his mind raced with possibilities.

"Maybe there's really a way to go home after all."

****

The church had been marked off with bright caution tape. John Tindilli pulled a long piece of it away from the door, letting it drop to the ground.

"There was something else here." Louis said absently, squinting at a darkened area next to the doors. "I can sense it, someone else was here besides the murderer," and that was when his vision blurred and he felt the terror of a soul, from inside the church, but it was fading.

"I've got to get in there fast," he urged Tindilli. "I can feel it, the agony of the priest, but it's nearly gone."

He rushed inside ahead of Tindilli, Bruce firmly perched on his shoulder. He passed several police officers and Detectives working over the site and taking pictures. Their individual auras stood out to him, the mix of colors momentarily confusing him on top of the agony he felt from the priest.

"I'm really slipping." He thought to himself, immediately taking control of his ability to see people by their halo of character and shutting it off so quickly his head hurt.

He could feel the pain of the priest more strongly the closer he got to the confessionals. The doors were intact, but when he peeked inside Father Benjamin's cubicle he saw how the wall separating the tiny rooms had been tore apart, and noted how torn up the body was. In spite of the mortal injuries the man had sustained, there was hardly any blood anywhere to be seen.

"Well, what's your take on it?" Tindilli asked, coming up behind him. "Ya think Christopher Lee is on a rampage, or is it one of those new sparkling guys?"

"Yeah, you're right, not much blood at all," Louis responded, ignoring his comment but not the meaning behind it.

In his mind's eye Louis saw the past from the remnants of the priest's soul. It was a young boy, a child. Somehow the boy had done the damage he saw; transformed into something incredibly vicious and committed the murder. Killed and even drank the blood of his victim.

It was a demon, a cambion similar to himself but something about him was different, and very powerful in spite of his size.

The vision staggered him and he stumbled back from the confessional door, hitting into Tindilli. His stomach felt as if it was doing flip-flops in his belly and he fought the urge to wretch.

"Hey, are you okay?" He asked, steadying Louis by putting his hands on his shoulders. "Do you need to sit down?"

"No, I'm okay. Sorry, just sort of got taken by surprise for a second there." Louis shrugged off the disorientation he felt from seeing the image of the young demon and shook his head. "It was a demon, but not a normal demon." He whispered to Tindilli.

"C'mon, let's get out of here so we can talk." Tindilli ushered him away, nodding to the other officers present as they made their way back outside.

They got to the stairs outside and Louis pulled Tindilli aside to stand in the shadow of a pillar at the entrance to the building.

"It's a kid, a young boy," Louis said in a rush. "He's like me, but there's something different about him too. I don't understand it, the scent, even the vision. The image I was able to get of him from the final vestiges of the priest, it was blurry but clear enough. I wasn't able to talk to Father Benjamin, his soul was long gone, as if it were taken abruptly. But there was enough of it lingering for me to see what happened."

"A kid did that?" Tindilli stared at Louis in shock.

"Not just any kid," Louis lit a cigarette and shook his head. "He's like me, not exactly like me, but like me."

"So he's a demon? How could he be in a church?" He looked at Louis, confused. "Why would he kill a priest?"

"Well, that's where I'm finding things to be a little sketchy." Louis said flatly.

"Let's get out of here and talk over coffee." Tindilli said after seeing two crime scene investigators pull up in a van. "There's a vender down the street, we can grab something there. It should be far enough away for us to be able to talk."

Louis shrugged and followed him down the stairs.

By the smell alone Louis could tell that the coffee was strong, but Bruce still climbed down his arm to take a sip of it. He cackled in approval, nodding vigorously, so Louis bought him his own small cup.

The three moved over to a newspaper machine next to a bus stop, Louis across from Tindilli, with Bruce standing on the machine drinking his coffee.

"Coffee's pretty good." Louis said looking at the vending truck. He noticed what looked like a homeless man sitting on the curb in front of it.

"Yeah, strong enough to keep me going this morning." Tindilli said, pulling a fresh cigar from his jacket pocket. "I need this."

"Hold on a minute." Louis walked back to the vending truck and bought a hotdog and soda. He walked over to the homeless man and handed it to him, along with the change he had from the twenty dollar bill he'd used to pay for it. "Here, you look like you can use a snack."

The man turned and smiled at Louis.

"Thank you." The man's voice was soft but strong.

"Have a good day." Louis said, turning to walk away.

"You know, it was really Diane, Louis. It really was her." The man said when Louis had gotten as far as the vending truck. "Sometimes you just need to have a little faith. There's more than just evil on the streets of the city."

Taken aback, Louis stopped mid-stride and spun around, and though his words still rang in Louis ears, the man was gone.

"What....." He was so shocked he couldn't even find the words, didn't know what to say. He looked up at the sky, closed his eyes and smiled, grateful for the gift he'd been given. Truly seeing Diane again was more than he ever expected. "Thanks."

I wish we had more than a few minutes together Sweetheart, but I'm grateful for the little time we had. Louis said to himself.

"Hey Louis, what are you doing?" Tindilli said impatiently. "I thought we were going to talk about the case not stare at the clouds."

Jarred back to reality, he went back over to Bruce and Tindilli, shaking his head.

"Did you just see what happened?" He asked Tindilli incredulously.

"What? You walked away." He replied, looking confused. "I called over to you because you were just standing there looking up."

Bruce pulled his head out of the coffee he

was drinking and looked at Louis, his tiny head turning sideways as if he were as baffled as Tindilli.

"Okay, no problem." Louis looked back over to where the homeless man was sitting and grinned. *"There's no point in adding to what's going on by trying to explain that I thought I was hallucinating when I saw my dead wife a little while ago, but then a homeless guy that no one saw but me confirmed that it was really her. Maybe it was an angel?"* He put the question aside and turned back to Tindilli who stared at him expectantly.

"Now, about this 'kid' you said you saw?" Tindilli asked.

"Well, he's definitely not a normal kid, he's half demon, but I don't think his mother was totally human either, I just can't place what it is." Louis said, trying not to sound as perplexed as he felt. "I've got a little research to do on this, but as for the priest, now that's a weird thing."

"What do you mean weird?" Tindilli made a face at him. "He got torn to shreds. It wasn't even messy because he had most of his blood sucked out of him like he got worked over by a fucking vampire. That's not just weird it's pretty fucked up considering it happened in a church too!"

"Yeah, but the guy was a child molester." Louis looked at Tindilli sternly. "Check his background. I bet there's something about him messing with kids somehow, whether it was altar boys, kids in a youth group he ran or even a basketball team. There's got to be something. I felt it. He was a very guilty man but couldn't even face his own sins. His parish was weak because of him."

"Okay, but what does that prove?" Tindilli said cynically. "Why would a demon want to kill a man that was doing terrible things here on earth? Wouldn't that be a good thing?"

"Well, you're right. He was doing the work of the devil." Louis raised his brow. "The devil wouldn't send someone to kill him unless he wanted the evil of his soul for something. He must have needed the man for some reason, because a priest doing what he was doing is really super good business for the Devil and sort of a slap in the face to God. Demons like B'lial, they use souls as currency. The more evil souls, the more powerful you are, the higher you are in the pits and in the eyes of the Master."

"Okay, I get it." Tindilli nodded and stubbed out his cigar. "I'll look into his background and get back to you with anything I learn. But if you find out anything, and I mean anything, about this please keep me informed. If there's a kid doing this, demon or not, we've got to put a stop to it as soon as we can before more people die."

"We're a team John," Louis said shaking his hand. "No matter what, we're always a team."

"We're not just a team Louis, we're family." Tindilli said, smacking him on the back. "You too Bruce," he laughed, pointing at the raven who nodded at them both. "And don't ever forget it."

FOUR

When Christian woke from his nap it was already early evening. He could see from his bedroom window that the sun had already started to go down and it was a little chilly in his room.

"Why is it every time I wake up from a nap I feel like I'm starving?" He said, kicking out of bed. "Feels like it's going to be a pizza night. Maybe even some beer if I can make myself look old enough, not that getting carded would be a problem; I can make whoever cards me see one. It's all just bullshit." Christian sounded jovial. "I don't just say bullshit, I create it." He laughed to himself and went downstairs.

He thought back to a time when he'd actually gone into a place called 'Dave's Tavern' and altered his features enough to bear the resemblance of a man old enough to drink. He made sure he was muscular and had perfect hair and even formed the tattoo of a heart on his bicep with the word 'MOM' written in it.

"The 'badboy' always has a good time and gets the girl in the end." He thought to himself. *"It'll be just the movies."*

Christian had hours of fun that night playing pool, drinking and mingling with people that had no idea of the evil in their midst. He was a target for every woman there, and a subject to be sized up by every man. Being judged a threat by some of the men, he avoided confrontations with sarcastic humor and allowed himself to lose several games of pool just to make the night interesting and not filled with brawls.

Eventually he picked up a woman in her mid thirties. He thought she was the prettiest of the bar whores present, with long hair the fake blonde color that looked more yellow than blonde, and eyes that were encircled with so much darkness that someone should have taken the mascara away from her.

Her name was Connie. He didn't

remember her last name or she ever even told him what it was. She did mention that she worked in a daycare center.

"I wonder how she looks at work?" Christian chuckled, *"Maybe the kids do her make-up."*

Everything was going well until he brought her home after the bar closed. He expected that, in fact, hoped for it. She saw his parents and the horror visible in her expression was priceless to Christian. Like the Sanders, they were no longer alive, but unlike them they'd gone beyond just smelling horrible.

Christian showed her who he really was at that moment, and the crazed look on her face made the night of drinking more than worth it. Connie didn't even have a chance to get more than a muffled scream out.

Needless to say, the young lady never left the house alive.

"That was a tasty morsel," he laughed to himself.

The house phone was in the kitchen, and he was making his way to it to call for take-out until he noticed another body sitting in the recliner across from the couch where his foster parents sat.

"Hello Christian." Elizabeth said, sounding annoyed. "I see you're up to your old tricks again."

****

Father Frederick Volip had just finished

cleaning up after having breakfast with the residents of the shelter at St. Joe's. He snacked on the leftover buttered toast while folding up the chairs and setting them against the wall of the room where they all ate their meals.

"Wasting food is a sin after all," he said quietly, patting his ample belly with the palm of his hand and downing the last piece of toast with a cup of coffee. He walked upstairs to the small office he kept behind the main altar of the church, intending on checking over the books to make sure all the bills had been paid on time for the month so far, but then he remembered he wanted to light a candle for Jack, a member of the shelter that had been murdered recently, and Father Carmichael, a fellow priest and also a victim as well.

He got up to the main floor of the church, blessed himself when he reached the altar, then walked around it to the rack of candles that lined the wall in front of the confessionals.

"Father Volip?"

He spun around to the sound of his name being called just as he'd lit the second candle. A man was standing directly behind him. Father Volip was perplexed when he didn't recognize his face.

The man was large, as if he were an athlete, and tall. *"He's got to be at least six-feet tall,"* he mused, and there was something familiar about him but Volip couldn't place what it was. The man was wearing a brown leather overcoat and leather gloves. The overcoat added to Volip's perception of the man's size because of the width of his shoulders. His face was thin and angular, with a narrow chin and piercing green eyes. His dark hair was short and slicked back to reveal a slight widow's peak.

"Yes, that's me. What can I do for you?" Volip asked, stepping forward and holding out his hand.

The man shook hands with him and smiled. He had a firm grip and a hand that was so large Volip's own disappeared within it.

"I read in the newspaper that there were some murders associated with this shelter recently and I thought I may be able to help." He slipped his hand into his overcoat and produced a business sized envelope from it. He smiled and handed it to Father Volip. "I'd like to make a donation. It's rather sizeable, but I imagine you'd like to update all the locks so they're a bit more modern and perhaps even have an alarm system put in. You can use whatever is left over for anything the place needs."

Father Volip took the envelope and audibly gasped. It was as least an inch thick and full of hundred dollar bills.

"I don't understand." He said

dumbfounded, doubtfully looking up to face the man. "We don't usually receive donations in this fashion, if any at all. Is this from a legitimate business? If the funds are questionable in any way I can't accept them."

"I assure you, the money is clean. I've recently inherited a great deal of property and a very large sum." He grinned and thought of the pit in Dantalian's realm, with its accumulation of stolen property. "One of my relatives used to hoard all sorts of trinkets and antiques, picking them up from various outings over the years. As it turned out much of them are worth money. I've taken to selling some of them off to provide you with some funding. After hearing the hardship your organization has had I thought I may be able to help. It feels like the right thing for me to do. There should be enough there to help cover some bills and maybe even provide some new furnishings for the shelter."

"There most certainly is. I don't think I've ever seen so many hundred dollar bills before." Volip said, excitedly thumbing through the cash. "Well, God bless you. I don't know how to thank you. This will do the shelter a world of good! What's your name?"

"My name is Daniel, Daniel Smith." He said shaking the priest's hand again. "I hope to be around to help out as much as possible."

"Do you live in the city?" The priest

asked.

"I have a suite at the Paramount right now. I enjoy the view." He nodded and smiled. "I grew up here and in the surrounding area."

"I can count this out and write out a proper receipt if you give me a moment." Volip said hopefully. "I have a small office right over there." He pointed to the closed door at the rear of the altar.

"No need, honestly." He held up a hand. "Just put it to good use. I'll see you again sometime soon."

With that said, Obscure left the church, heading toward the Hudson, where he fondly remembered walking as a young boy. He liked the bitter chill of the winds that came off the water even in warm weather. The smell of trash was gone, the area having been cleaned up of late as had much of Hell's Kitchen.

"It's almost a shame things have been cleaned up." He said aloud. "I was so used to it the other way, when I fought with rats and stepped through refuse just to take a walk in the evening."

Obscure was happy, an unfamiliar yet welcome emotion. The smile that lit up his clean features was something he didn't recognize when he spied his own reflection on the window of a parked car he passed by while walking.

The face, ruggedly handsome, was truly

his own, but he still wasn't used to seeing it, and had no idea what his own expressions would look like.

The act of transforming into a human form was invigorating. He had come resemble what he would have looked like had he the same traits as his brother Louis from birth.

"This is what I should have looked like, who I should have been all along." He said aloud, his voice no longer carrying bitterness, holding his head up high.

He was free, freer than he'd ever been before. It was as if he'd gotten a second chance, and in a way he felt like an excited child. Obscure had power, Hell and earth, more money then he'd ever know what to with, and a shadow that would take him anywhere his heart desired.

"Maybe I'll buy a car just for the sake of having one!" Obscure laughed lightly and headed back to his hotel room.

****

"Now what's a girl like you doing in a place like this?" Christian sounded surprised. "I'd heard you'd been killed, or rather, destroyed as happens with our kind."

"What's that old saying, 'The news of my demise is a bit premature'?" She flashed him a perfect toothy smile and stood up from the recliner. "Now I want an answer. What are you doing here? You're the one that killed the priest this morning. Why? What was he to you?"

Elizabeth was dressed as if she were on her way to a club. She wore a skintight black mini-dress with high spiked heels and a thin choker with a black rose on it around her throat.

"What's it to you?" Christian squinted angrily at her, his skin swelling, body growing slightly with the change he barely held back from. "I don't have to answer to you."

"Yeah, I know, because I'm not your mother, but I do know who she is." Elizabeth narrowed her eyes at him. "And if you want to change go right ahead, you don't frighten me. I've beaten some pretty powerful demons in my day."

Christian gave in, not caring whether or not she knew because she couldn't stop him anyway. His body relaxed and he just stood there.

"Well, it's sort of a favor for my mother. She's actually having me do it as a favor she owes someone else." He said sounding flustered. "That's all I know about it."

"I supposed it's B'lail, isn't it?" Her eyes widened when she said his name. "It's about him isn't it?"

"B'ial? No, B'lial was destroyed a week or so ago." He replied, shaking his head. "Really messy too from what I was told, and it happened in the pits."

"What!" She shouted without realizing it. "Destroyed? By who?"

"His sons." Christian smiled wickedly. "He had two, you know, they were twins. You were really close to one of them, right?" He smiled at her mockingly. "B'lial wanted you to seduce him and bend him to your will."

Elizabeth ignored the boy's taunting comment; back-stepped and nearly wound up falling back into the recliner again.

"He did it, he really did it!" She thought to herself excitedly. *"I'd hoped that he would never have met his brother though; such a tragic man. At least they worked together somehow to make it happen. I'll have to look in on him soon to see how he's doing now that he's free of B'lial."*

"Now tell me," Christian said, sounding more than a little annoyed. "What are you doing here in my house?"

"I've come here to stop you from killing more people." She gestured to the couple 'seated' at the couch. "Good or bad, you've no right to kill anyone. You're no judge, jury and executioner. I don't care if it's for your mother. Hell, that's all the more reason why you have to stop." Elizabeth said angrily. "She's doubtless up to no good, and I've dealt with her enough over the years to know that for a fact. I can't let her get what she wants."

"If I say no, how do you plan on stopping

me?" He asked deviously, wringing his hands together.

"I'll kill you myself, and then deal with your mother in my own fashion." She said sternly, eyes glowing with anger. The sound of the skin on her hands tearing open broke the eerie silence that had formed between them as long sharp claws extended themselves from her fingertips.

"Let me get this straight. I'm not supposed to kill anyone but you can kill me if I don't do what I'm being told?" He shook his head angrily. "Now that's bullshit! You can't just come into my home and tell me something like that. It's just not fair." Christian had a devilish look on his face. "That must be why my mother warned me about you. She didn't think you were really dead."

"She may be a bitch, but she's a smart bitch, I'll grant her that." Elizabeth said, half-heartedly swiping her hand at Christian and nearly clawing through his clothes. "Let's not make this too difficult. Make your choice, fight or end it!"

"I always do what Mom tells me to do." Christian smiled wickedly.

"It doesn't matter what she told you to do, I'll tear you apart!" Elizabeth said, her body beginning to transform into that of a demon.

"That would also explain why she gave me this." Christian pulled a small hand mirror out of his pocket and flung it at Elizabeth, all the while reciting a prayer to the Master himself. The mirror turned dark as his words became deeper and louder.

Swiping at him again, Elizabeth suddenly found herself unable to reach him. It took a moment for her to realize she was shrinking, being pulled toward the mirror as it flew toward her, flipping end over end like a black hole in the air.

"No!" Was the last word she could shout before being sucked inside the mirror, where she would remain trapped, helpless until she gathered enough strength to break free.

"Well, mom did say you were vein, so it only seemed fitting when she made this mirror especially for you." Christian laughed.

The mirror flashed brightly, then went dark and fell on the floor without shattering.

"Now I think it's about time that I finally ordered dinner. I may even celebrate with extra cheese, sausage and pepperoni in spite of the heartburn I get from it." He said kneeling down to pick up the mirror. He could see Elizabeth's face in it as he dropped it on the end table next to the recliner. "This should be a good enough prison for someone that betrayed B'lial, even if it only lasts for a little while!" He said to Elizabeth. "Just be lucky Lily didn't make it a brittle little mirror, prone to shattering. I'll figure out what to do with you after I eat. It's been a long day."

Christian turned back around to head for the kitchen and the phone.

FIVE

The phone rang and Louis jumped.

He'd fallen asleep sitting back in a leather recliner. He was reading in his study after a long day of searching, trying to get a lead on the priest's murder. When Louis finally got home after coming up empty he just crashed with 'Quest of the Spider' an old 'Doc Savage' pulp novel he'd bought at a used book store. He wanted dinner but there was nothing worth eating in the fridge so he resigned himself to going out for breakfast with Bruce in the morning.

The phone sounded like a blaring siren

ringing in his ears. He abruptly dropped the book and swung his arm over to the end table next to the chair and grabbed the phone.

"Yeah?" he said, fumbling with the phone for a second.

"Louis, it's John." Louis heard Tindilli sigh heavily. "We got a bad one here."

"What's going on, what happened?" He asked, rubbing his eyes with his free hand and stifling a yawn.

"A young couple and a pizza delivery boy, looks like the same thing as the priest." Tindilli said. "I could really use your help here as soon as you can."

"I'll be right there, just give me the address." Louis ran his hand through his hair and memorized the address Tindilli recited into the phone.

Louis sat back in the chair heavily and lit a cigarette after hanging up.

"Bruce!" He shouted. "C'mon Bruce, we've gotta meet Tindilli!"

A heartbeat later the raven flew into the room, a sheet of paper hanging from his feet.

"What do you have there?" Louis snatched the paper from him and the raven flew around behind him to land on his shoulder.

Louis read the paper and laughed out loud.

NO

FOOD
HUNGRY

"Yeah, I know there's no food in the house." He laughed and crumpled up the paper, tossing it in the trash. "I was going to take you out for breakfast until Tindilli called." He said walking downstairs. "The sun's barely up, so we're both going to have to settle for nothing until we're done at the crime scene."

Louis grabbed his black duster from the coat rack and slipped it over his shoulders. Bruce, already cranky, cackled, jumped up and hovered there until he could return to his shoulder again.

"Hang on tight, this is the first time I've tried doing this since we were in Hell with Obscure." Louis winked at the raven and imagined the address Tindilli gave him, picturing the numbers in his head as a reference point. "Shadow," he whispered, and suddenly liquid darkness spilled out of him, slowly coalescing to form into his pitch-black, featureless, mirror image on the wall in front of him. "You know where to take us, let's go."

Without saying another word, Louis walked right into his shadow, vanishing in the blackness. He felt the familiar icy chill of the darkness, the transition between one place and another and smiled to himself.

"I'm glad this still works." He thought to himself. *"It's going to save me a lot of mileage on*

my old MG."

At the front gate of the Sanders' property, Louis' shadow appeared and he stepped out of it, Bruce still on his shoulder. The swirling darkness of his shadow returned to him and he opened the wooden gate.

"Look around Bruce, see if you can find anything to help us out." He said. Bruce leaped into the air, flying low around to the back of the property.

That was when he noticed a uniformed officer standing on the front steps do a double-take and look at him strangely.

Louis thought fast, and quickly turned around, acting as if he was looking for something in the street.

"Officer, did you see my cab?" He said making his way to the porch. "It was just there a second ago." He forced himself to sound annoyed. "I even gave him a few bucks to wait for me."

The officer looked even more confused, but shook his head hesitantly.

"No, I didn't see any cab." He stuttered a nervous reply.

"Tindilli still inside?" Louis said, flashing his PI badge.

The officer nodded and opened the door for him.

"Louis?" Tindilli called out, meeting him at the door. He handed him a pair of surgical gloves to wear. "C'mon, ya gotta see this." He pulled Louis over to the couch in the living room where the Sanders still sat. "You can see the slash marks on each of the victims, but look at their throats, the marks."

"It looks like a vague outline." Louis said. "Like mouth, or rather lip prints."

"There wasn't even an attempt made to clean off the marks." Tindilli shook his head. "The kid must be pretty confident that we won't be able to find him if he's that careless."

"If he can alter his appearance he'd be right." Louis agreed.

The souls of the deceased were long gone, he could sense that, but there was a trace of someone else still lingering there.

"Where's the other victim? I think I got something." He said to Tindilli trying to hold onto what he was seeing.

"He's in the kitchen," he said, taking him there. "It looks like he was killed while putting the pizza down on the table. Crazy, huh?"

"Yeah," he agreed. "He was probably told to come around back, and thought nothing of it." Louis gestured to the kitchen door. "He wouldn't see the other victims in the living room that way."

The body of a man in his early twenties was sprawled over the back of a chair at the kitchen table. The pizza box was on the table directly in front of him. It was half-empty.

Again Louis got the vague impression, a vision of a young dark haired boy, and the sensation of terrible pain from the victim. Then it was gone.

"You're right." Louis looked at Tindilli. "Same kid, though he used a knife this time and not his hands, or claws from the way it looked at the church."

"No blood anywhere either. Victims in the living room have been dead for a couple of days, but this one couldn't have been here longer than a few hours, maybe sometime late last night."

"And he made sure all the pizza didn't go to waste." Louis shook his head, aggravated at the thought of it. "Did the kid actually live here?"

"Yeah, the crew is upstairs right now going through his room. There isn't much more than a couple of pictures and some clothes though." Tindilli said, annoyed. "Here, check it out." He handed Louis a picture with the boy he recognized from his visions standing with the Sanders in front of a museum. "I've got a call out to Youth and Family Services to get any information they may have on the kid."

Louis looked at the picture and studied the face of the young boy. It was definitely the same boy from his visions; the same one in the minds of all the victims thus far. It was so odd looking at the picture, seeing such a young boy that resembled someone in a commercial for a video game or popular toy and know that he was a demon and a murderer.

"If he's a cambion and he's been doing this for a while he'll have ways to make new identities, methods to pass himself off safely. So even if they have something on him we won't have much of a real history." Louis thought for a minute then returned the frame to Tindilli. "He's probably been all over the state, or even country. There's no way to know for sure."

"He didn't beat us yet. I'll send out the information we get from Family Services and see if we can get any matches in the tri-state area and if not I'll move further out." He put the picture on the table. "I'll also put out an APB for a kid fitting his description too, so if he shows up anywhere we'll get a call. If he's like you, can the two of you be related somehow? You know, like you are with Obscure?"

"If B'lial had any other kids that were floating around on earth I'm sure he would have thrown that at me in a heartbeat, just to taunt me." His eyes narrowed, "He'd brag about having a son that would kill for him."

The coroner ducked his head in the room.

"You guys need more time in here?" He asked.

"No, it's okay, we'll be leaving soon." Tindilli slipped a cigar out of his pocket and gestured toward the back door. "Let's go outside where we can talk without anyone hearing."

Louis pulled off the surgical gloves, wadded them up and put them in his coat pocket.

"This entire situation really just pisses me off." He said angrily. "I thought I was done with the whole 'demon fighting' thing and now this has to happen! I mean really, what the fuck? Can I ever get a break?"

"We'll get him Louis." Tindilli reassured him while lighting his cigar. "Demon or not, we're good at what we do."

"What if things were always this way and we just never knew it?" Louis asked.

"What do you mean?" Tindilli puffed away at his cigar and turned away from him, "Demons committing crimes, murdering people?"

"That's exactly what I mean. We would have had no way of knowing before." Louis lit a cigarette and rubbed his eyes. "Finding out about B'lial and my true heritage may have opened up a whole can of worms."

Tindilli spun around to face Louis.

"Even if it did, we always caught them before, we still will now. Hell, it may even be easier now that we've got you on our side to fill in the blanks we never knew about."

"You're right about that," Louis said, searching the sky for Bruce. "Though I hope ultimately I'm wrong about it."

"I know this may be a tough subject to think about, but if you and Diane ever had a child, would it be like you?"

"Yeah, though I guess the bloodline on my father's side would be more diluted. Any baby we had would have a darkness inside it, however slight, something from B'lial." Louis' eyes suddenly glowed red with anger. "What if Diane didn't lose our baby? What if B'lial took it somehow? This killer, this kid, could be my own son!"

"Louis, you're reaching pretty far with that." Tindilli said skeptically, putting his hand on Louis' shoulder to calm him down. "I seriously doubt the killer could be your son. You'd know, somehow you'd just know."

"No, hear me out." His eyes widened and he stubbornly pulled away from his ex-partner. "B'lial was powerful enough to do what he did to me; the whole thing with the cemetery and my mother's grave. I told you what happened, what I saw and heard, and it was all an illusion. Even Elizabeth and how she had a store that never really existed. Why couldn't he make it seem like Diane lost a baby? He's got that kind of power. I always suspected that he was behind her getting cancer in the first place I just never talked about it."

"Louis-" Tindilli tried to cut him off, but his eyes got wild and he raised his voice in frustration and anger.

" We're not talking about regular people here we're talking about some very powerful beings that are way beyond us in terms of what they can do, and how evil they can be. Think about it! Just the fact that my father existed is enough to boggle the mind!"

"I understand what you're saying, but honestly, I think you're way off base here." Tindillis insisted. "I know you're very close to everything that's happened, and I'm sure it's overwhelming, but I need you to calm down for a minute and think things out. Please, just a take a breath and relax."

Tindilli stood facing Louis, cigar trailing smoke from his mouth, hoping he'd listen.

Reluctantly, Louis put it all out of his head for a moment and thought of Diane; how she looked a couple of months pregnant and how they both had so much hope for a healthy baby and a normal life. It was his dream to have a family and grow old with Diane; someday becoming grandparents.

The images in his mind abruptly faded when he remembered that he just saw Diane, the feeling of her in his arms still lingering. If there was ever a baby she would have told him about it, especially if B'lial was somehow involved. She would never have left him in the dark about something so important to both of them.

"You're right John," Louis' voice lowered, his shoulders slumping in defeat. "I'm sorry. I'm just getting paranoid and crazy."

"We both are," Tindilli put his arm around Louis. "I wish things were easier for you. I still have a hard time believing what's happened over the past couple of years. The thought of Diane being gone and your father…" He let his words fade to avoid getting upset. He loved Louis and Diane as if they were his own children.

"I'm really sorry I went a little nuts there for a minute." Louis pulled away when he heard Bruce approaching. The raven cackled and landed on his shoulder. "I think I need to take a day off of all this, maybe just kick back."

"Have you heard anything from your sister-in-law, what was her name, Jean?" He said thoughtfully. "Maybe now would be a good time to see her."

"I wasn't able to get in touch with her for a while because of the whole B'lial situation. I'll give her a call when I get home, maybe make a trip into New Jersey to see her and Stephanie." Louis' face brightened.

SIX

The Paramount Hotel was a different world to 'Daniel Smith'. When he first saw it from the outside he was amazed at how it looked. The pale carved stone around the windows of the lower floors set it apart from other buildings and to him made it resemble something from a lost age, as if it were a place made for royalty to reside.

"The perfect place for me to live while I decide what to do next in my new life," he said aloud. "Without having to worry about age touching me, I have all the time in the world."

In many ways the hotel was the flipside to

what he had grown up in. The lobby was immaculate, even smelling fresh and clean, a far cry from the shelters and alleyways he'd been accustomed to. The people at the hotel were even happy to see him, though they had no idea who he was. He wasn't sure if he'd ever get used to that. The first time he walked in he had to suppress a smile, not wanting to look like a deprived child that was finally given a cookie.

'Daniel Smith' had become the name Obscure would answer to. He had successfully put away his memory of being 'Goliath' and 'Obie', vowing to never go by either name again. He set about enjoying his new life, which would be a balance between the chaos of Hell and an easier life on earth as a man. He knew it wouldn't be an easy task but he had to try and make it work.

While still in Dantalian's pit he discovered that finding his human side, his human body, was easier said than done. The transformation was excruciatingly painful at first, but as his thick, coarse, demon flesh tore open and fell away to be replaced by the smooth human skin under it, he reveled in the pain, thinking of it as a rebirth.

Pulling an old silver mirror from the pit, he looked himself over for the first time, amazed at how handsome he was as a human. He resembled his brother Louis, but there was a rougher edge to his features that his brother didn't have, and Daniel liked it.

"It can only get easier as time passes," he said aloud in the pit before willing the dark door of his shadow to open and transport him to the city he knew so well.

While on earth he wanted to have the life of a very well to do man, akin to his new life in Hell, where he had power and minions to do his bidding. He did everything he could to make it that way. Daniel even went so far as picking up a copy of his Social Security Card from the government office on West 48th Street. They had a record of his birth, or at least the day that he was found, and were able to give him a copy of that as well.

"I know this world too well to think I could survive the way I want to without having a true identity." He thought to himself while having a suit made at a tailor shop only a short cab ride away from the Paramount. *"My illusions would give me a fair life for a time, and I'm sure I'd enjoy it, but they are what they are; fake, lies masked in suggestion and trickery. I want things to be as real as possible. I want to experience everything I was denied my entire life, and live life as it should have been had I the good fortune of my twin."*

He bought a wallet from a small store after ordering several more suits of different colors and styles from the tailor shop. It was a smooth black leather tri-fold. He slid his new

Social Security Card in it, and as much cash that would fit with it still being able to fold closed and fit into his jacket pocket.

That was when he checked into the hotel, the place he had come to think of as paradise on earth. He was disappointed that he had to cast the illusion of having a credit card in order to stay there, but he knew he could get his own real one once he paid a local bank a visit and made a sizeable deposit.

Nothing was impossible anymore.

Money would never be a problem either. He had so much of it in Dantalian's pit that all he had to do was order his lower demons and imps to dig it out and bring it to him, which they were more than happy to do. As one of B'lial's underlings, Dantalian had been hoarding things for centuries, stealing from people as a means of causing anger and chaos in their lives. Louis had done him a huge favor by destroying the demon a short time ago. There was cash, jewelry, gold coins and a huge assortment of junk in the demon's pit of trinkets.

Donating some money to St. Joes, the shelter that had been such a big help to him a short time ago was the least he thought he could do. It was a way of saying 'thanks' and also a way to say goodbye to Jack, a man that never judged him by his looks and treated him as an equal even though he was a hulking brute swathed in gauze and heavy clothing.

"I wish you were here Jack, we'd have a lot of fun!" He said aloud as he approached the entrance to the hotel after leaving St. Joe's.

The bar at the Paramount was spotless. The lighting was dim but it enhanced the lighter colored interior, especially the circular lights hanging above the bar itself. He sat at the far end of the bar near empty bar, next to the entrance and facing the rest of the room. With his hearing as acute as it was he could already hear all the conversations around him, but watching made it real.

"My name is Rachael, what can I get for you this afternoon sir?" The barmaid was a beautiful brunette with soft features and a quiet voice. Her skin was so smooth looking she barely looked old enough to be standing behind the bar.

It was the first time he'd sat in a bar that wasn't full of loud drunk people fighting or trying to play pool when they could barely stand. He almost didn't know how to answer, and was embarrassed when he couldn't think of how to say what he wanted at first.

"I'd like a domestic beer, whatever you have on tap, and a shot of whiskey." Daniel said with a slight nod.

"Would you like me to list the brands, sir?" The barmaid asked.

"I'll leave that up to you." He smiled,

realizing that he'd found the perfect 'out' for not knowing the difference. "I trust your judgment."

"Okay, I'll surprise you." The barmaid winked at him and walked off.

Daniel looked around, still excited just to be there. When the barmaid returned she put both glasses down in front of him on a napkin and smiled again.

"I have a Brooklyn Ale for you," she pointed to the beer, "Brewed locally, and a shot of Hudson Single Malt Whiskey, also made locally. They both have excellent reviews."

"Well, thank you Rachael." He grinned and took a sip of the beer. "Nice," he said, enjoying the full, nutty flavor of the beer. It was much different from the canned beer he'd purchased in the past. There was no metallic taste and it was ice-cold.

"I'm glad you like it." Rachael said happily. "It's a favorite here."

Daniel took another sip before he lifted up the shot of whiskey. He looked at it for a moment before drinking it, noting that it was much darker in color compared to anything he had before. "It certainly looks good." He threw back the shot in a quick movement and was surprised at how smooth the flavor was. There was no harshness to it like the whiskey he'd had when he went out with Jack, who always remained sober because of his previous drinking problem. He laughingly couldn't imagine seeing a bottle of it wrapped in a brown paper bag. "Very good!" He said heartily. "I knew having you pick for me was the right thing to do."

"Well thank you," She smiled at him. "Would you like me to start a tab for you? If you're staying at the hotel I can just add it to your room. Either way is fine."

"Neither if you don't mind." He took out his wallet and handed her a fifty dollar bill. "Can you just give me another round of the same and keep the rest for yourself?"

"Why certainly," she replied, beaming at him. "Thank you very much."

He watched her walk off trying not to think about how pretty she was, how much he craved what he'd never had his entire life. Young women, old women, it never mattered, they always turned away from him with disgust in their eyes, or worse; fear.

"I hope you don't mind if I join you."

The voice he heard was throaty, sexy. He jerked his head around nervously to see who it came from because he never heard the woman come in the door, and knew he should have. There was a sudden thickness to the air and he felt her evil as his eyes met hers.

"Not at all," he replied as casually as he could, the sense of attraction toward her both strangely unexpected and overwhelming.

She was dressed in black, the darkness of her clingy dress only accenting her slim yet full figure. Her face was an oval accented by high cheekbones and dark, wide expressive eyes framed by long wavy black hair. Everything about her felt magnetic, enticing, from her scent to the way the light danced in her dark eyes.

"Do I know you?" Daniel asked, unable to take his eyes off of her. He tried to see her aura, but oddly enough, it was as if she had none.

"I doubt it, but I'm sure you've heard of me." She leaned forward and threw her hair back, exposing more of her face, more of her smile.

"I know we have much in common." Daniel leaned back, flustered. "I can feel it."

"My name is Lilith," she said, voice lowered to a whisper, "And I am the first woman. I will always be the first woman, banished from Paradise, trapped in Hell, only able to escape by bonding with it and giving up a part of myself."

Daniel remembered the stories of Lilith he'd been told growing up. B'lial had even mentioned her from time to time. *"She's like me,"* he thought, *"Rejected for nothing more than existing, being independent, being who she is. I can't imagine why that would be such a horrible thing."*

"Do you know who I am?" He asked timidly.

"I'd know a son of B'lial anywhere," she flashed her eyes at him and reached out to put her hand on his, "but you, you're not just his son, you were the forsaken one, just as I was. We have much in common, you and I."

Daniel's hand felt warm where she touched it. A woman had never reached out to touch him like that before. He liked the feeling, but wasn't sure he could trust it.

"Yes we do." He said. "Why are you here? Why did you want to meet me of all people?"

"In spite of the difficulties in your life, you fought against everything and came away from it powerful and triumphant. To me, that's very admirable, and a man I needed to meet. You destroyed your own father, your creator, a feat I wish I could have done countless centuries ago. What do you call yourself now?"

"My name is Daniel Smith." He replied with conviction.

"Well, I'm very pleased to meet you, Daniel." She said, holding out her other hand. He shook it gently, a persistent question fighting to find a voice inside him.

"So you knew B'lial?" He asked, pulling his hand away from hers, trying to put his desire for her out of his head.

"It was B'lial who rescued me when I was thrown from the gates of Paradise. He showed me how to survive, taught me things that I would have never known otherwise." Her eyes softened and she smiled at him. "Could I do any less to help his son?"

"I know of this world, having grown up in it. I don't need help." He said confidently. "I've done very well since B'lial's end, and I plan to be even more successful now that I reside in both worlds."

"Yes you certainly have done well, but there are things you have yet to experience that I can help you with, things that we can share and enjoy together." Lilith reached out for his hand again. He didn't pull away. Instead, he let his finger wrap into hers, taking great pleasure in how good it felt to hold the hand of such a beautiful woman. "I can show you a world you never even knew existed and bring you to the heights of pleasure only the sweetest of dreams can express."

Daniel felt drawn to her even more then he did before. It was as if time had stopped in the bar, and it was just the two of them sitting there next to each other. Lilith reached toward his face with her other hand and lightly traced his lips with her index finger.

Their eyes locked onto each other again, and Daniel Smith was lost.

SEVEN

Louis held the button down on the butter machine while Stephanie turned his bucket of popcorn. The smell of butter flavored oil made his mouth water, and he craved a cigarette that he wouldn't be able to have until the movie was over and he was outside.

"Louis you're worse than a kid. If you add anymore to that bucket you're gonna get sick." Jean said standing behind them. "I can hear your arteries screaming from here." She had an overflowing bucket herself which she planned on sharing with Stephanie, but there was hardly any butter on it and only a dash of salt. In her other hand was the torn tickets and a large drink.

"Popcorn has always been a weakness of mine since I was a kid. I can't go to a movie without a big bucket all to myself." Louis laughed. "And even though I know this isn't real butter, I don't care, it tastes great!"

Louis' hearing, enhanced as it was, involuntarily picked up the scuffling sound of roaches nearby, a lot of them. He could hear them close to his feet, climbing up the inside of the counter, all over, waiting to feast on anything they could find. Some of them were so hungry they didn't want to wait for the shroud of darkness to hide their gorging. Their communication between each other sounded gross to him, like rhythmic high-pitched gurgles and squeaks.

For a split second Louis lost himself in their resonance, but then Stephanie snapped him back to reality and he was able to tone down his own hearing in order to ignore the gross noise the roaches made.

"Are you done yet?" Stephanie asked with a giggle, noting how soggy the popcorn was beginning to look.

He shook his head to get the idea of the bugs being so close out of his mind and looked at his niece with a nervous grin.

"Shake the bucket a little to make sure things move around a little bit." He replied, looking down at the mess of butter flavored oil and popcorn. When he was satisfied with the mix, he nodded to Stephanie. "Now just make sure you grab a ton of napkins, I'm gonna need them. This stuff is going to be really greasy and I don't want to get any in my beard or on my clothes." The aroma of the popcorn made his mouth water.

"Bruce would have loved this." He thought to himself when he remembered how the raven helped him polish off a bag of popcorn the last time they watched a movie on television.

Stephanie grabbed him a small stack of napkins and handed him his soda. Then they all headed away from the concession stand to the theater where their movie would be starting soon.

"I'm so glad you called, I missed you so much." She said, her face lit with excitement as she popped a straw into the lid of his drink.

"I've missed you guys too! I can't even tell you how much." He said, finally feeling safe enough to say it since B'lial was destroyed.

"It's so strange, not having to look over my shoulder every minute," he thought. *"I bet there are Imps somewhere in the theater. Probably Zax and his group, annoying people and stealing whatever little things they could get their hands on. If they know I'm here they'll think twice about sticking around."*

"I've wanted to see this movie ever since I heard it was being made!" Stephanie smiled and took the soda he carried so she could hold his hand and pull him in the direction of the theater. "I've read all the books and they were great."

"Yeah, I guess sparkling vampires and underage wizards in the same film at the same time can only be box office gold these days." He chuckled looking at Jean who had an annoyed smile on her face.

"She hasn't stopped talking about it since you called two days ago." She sighed, falling in behind Stephanie and next to Louis. "I'm so glad you called when you did. We were really starting to get worried about you, especially after you resigned from the force. Law enforcement was your life."

"I guess I needed a change. I'm fine though, honestly, just incredibly busy these days." He gave her a serious look. "Staying occupied has been a big help to me, and being a private investigator is a much more involved job because I'm basically doing everything myself. Sometimes I get called in to help the local PD on a case here and there too, so I still see my old friends a lot more than I expected."

"John must be happy about that; you're like a son to him." Jean said.

"So he always tells me." Louis laughed, surprised at how happy he honestly felt. "It's been too long since I was able to just kick back and go to a movie with two of my favorite relatives. We might have to make this a monthly trip, if not more than that."

"That would be fine with me," Stephanie said, squinting in the darkness to try to find seats for them all. "I love hanging out with you, Uncle Louis."

Louis eventually spotted a bunch of empty seats in the center row near the front, and ushered them to it.

"This is great!" Stephanie bounced up in her seat which was between Jean and Louis. "We're really close."

"Keep it down, the previews are gonna start!" Her mother snapped.

Louis couldn't believe he'd driven to New Jersey to see them. The traffic was terrible, and he had to leave Bruce behind, but it was well worth it. Tindilli was right, as usual. He needed some time away from everything, even if it was just an afternoon and a matinee with dinner afterwards.

It had been over a year since the last time he'd seen Jean and Stephanie. Other than an occasional phone call or card he'd had no contact with them. He missed the two of them a great deal and was surprised to see how much bigger, more grown up Stephanie had become in such a short time. When he thought he'd never be able to see them again because of his father it hurt him more than he wanted to admit to himself. He'd already lost too much when Diane died. Stephanie reminded him of what he thought Diane was like as a child, and Jean, Diane's older sister, she resembled her a little and was fun to spend time with.

He sat there, enjoying the popcorn and trying to follow the movie that he considered a comedy even though it was supposed to be anything but that. Mostly he enjoyed the company. Louis got so involved that the thought of a cigarette didn't even cross his mind while the movie was showing.

When the film ended on a cliffhanger a little over two hours later, Stephanie was angry but hopeful about the promise of a sequel.

"We have to go see it when it comes out," she said urgently.

"Well, let me know when it comes out and we'll go." Louis looked at Jean and she nodded to him.

"Sure," she said, "Just go easier on the popcorn. I don't want you having a heart attack, especially since you picked up your smoking habit again." She had an annoyed expression on her face.

"I'll be fine. I don't do it as much as I used to." He shrugged, wishing he could explain to her that he was not prone to diseases anymore and was for all intents and purposes immortal, but the less she knew about the abilities he had by being half demon the better.

"It's early," Stephanie said, walking backwards to face them while they walked outside. "Can we still get dinner?"

"Absolutely." Louis said. "I can use a good steak and from what I remember there's a little place nearby that I used to frequent with your Aunt Diane when we were still dating."

"Ah, I remember." Jean smiled. "The place with the Shamrock on the sign, I can't think of the name of it."

"It's-" Louis was abruptly cut off by the loud chirp of his cell phone. He saw Tindilli's number flash on the screen and sighed. "I have to get this," he looked at Jean apologetically.

"Go ahead," she replied, holding her daughters hand.

"Yeah John?" He said, stepping away from them. "What's goin' on?"

"Hey, I think we have a lead on the kid." Tindilli sounded tired. "A call just came in from Youth and Family Services. They just got a call about a young boy, just showed up at St. Joe's shelter. And before you ask, yes, it's the same shelter we're both more than familiar with. They said he matched the photo we sent around except for his hair color, so we have to get over there and see if it's him before they send someone to pick him up."

"Where are you right now?" Louis asked. *"Why would he show up at the same shelter that Obscure and I stayed at? Is there really a connection to us or is it just a coincidence?"* The answers to his questions had to wait as Tindilli answered him.

"I'm driving to the shelter right now." He replied, "I want to check this out as soon as possible. If it's really him we can pull him out of there quick. I don't want anyone else getting killed."

"Okay, I'd meet you out front but I'll probably be there ahead of you." He said looking at Jean and shaking his head sadly.

"Be careful." Tindilli said before ending the call.

"Hey, I'm sorry but I'm going to have to get a rain check on dinner." Louis said, dropping his phone back in his pocket. "I've got an emergency in the city."

"Is everything okay?" Jean asked while Stephanie protested next to her.

"But it was supposed to be your day off." She said, running over to hug him.

"I know Steph, but you know I love you and I'll see you again soon." He looked at Jean. "Everything should be fine, if not you'll get a call. I've really got to run though."

"Don't be a stranger anymore," Jean said.

"I promise I won't." Louis nodded, "I'll make it a point to be around much more than I have."

He gave them both a quick hug and kiss and then ran in the direction of his car.

"I hope they don't actually follow me to my car, because I'm going to have to pick it up later. There's no time to drive there."

Louis had parked behind the theater, with the front of the car facing the back wall. As he neared the vehicle, he checked around to make sure there was no one around, then projected an image of St. Joe's in his mind and willed his shadow to appear on the wall. Without pause, he ran directly into it, vanishing into the black image.

He reappeared at the front gate to St. Joe's, suppressing a chill from the transition.

It was early evening and the sun had just started to go down. He could see the church had lights on somewhere inside and he could hear the sounds of a football game being broadcast on a television in the shelter below it. There was shouting, the men that lived there clearly getting into the game.

"I hope him being here is just a coincidence and nothing more." He said, racing up the church stairs. He quickly pulled out his phone and texted Tindilli that he was already inside to give him a heads up.

The doors were unlocked, as he thought they would be since there was a late mass every night of the week. He remembered as much from his time there as a resident in the shelter. When he stepped inside there were only a couple of lights on, so it was shadowy and quiet. In the distance he spotted the door to Father Volip's office. The light was on inside, so he headed in that direction.

"Volip must be in there," He thought, rushing over. *"Maybe the kid's with him. I hope the priest is okay. He seemed like a very sincere, nice man, I'd hate to see him hurt."*

He sensed the evil before reaching the altar. It was more powerful but matched what he'd sensed at the crime scenes with Tindilli. There was no longer any doubt in his mind as to whether or not the child was there or if he was who they were looking for.

As he got closer he could hear Volip talking, saying something about foster care.

"Father Volip?" Louis said, knocking on the doorframe while poking his head in. "Sorry to bother you sir, but I'm working with the police department, and I really need to speak to you right now about a very urgent matter." He pulled out his wallet and held up his badge so the priest could see it.

Volip was sitting behind his desk, with Christian sitting in a folding chair directly in front of it. The priest looked up at Louis. His eyes bulged with shock, and frantically he stood up.

"What's going on? Is someone hurt?" He asked, quickly coming around the desk. "Did something happen to one of the residents?"

Father Volip stopped when he was standing in front of Christian, who had sensed Louis arrival as quickly as Louis himself had known he was there. He glanced around Volip's leg and smiled wickedly at him.

Before Louis could respond, he saw the expression on Christian's face and stepped forward, eyes narrowing on the child.

"I guess you're here for me, and the proverbial cat's out of the bag." Christian said calmly. "Oh well, time for me to go!" He shoved the priest aside so hard he crashed into the wall and fell to the floor. Then he leapt straight at Louis, who had remained standing in the doorway.

Christian had begun transforming into his demonic form the moment he knew Louis was there. When he bounded toward him, his claws had already come out, so his hands were poised at Louis' throat.

Louis ducked low and grabbed hold of Christian's arms, twisting around to hurl him out of the room.

"Stay in here Father!" He called out to Volip, in case he was still conscious, and slammed the door.

Louis clenched his jaw angrily.

"Damn! It wasn't supposed to happen like this!" Holding out both of his hands, he froze time in the church. No one would know what was happening there until he wanted them too. It made the residents safe as well as Father Volip, who was still in his office.

"What have you done?" Christian shouted, hovering in the air above him, seeing the flames on the nearby candle stop flickering.

"I'm just making sure that no one else walks in on us." He gave Christian an angry look. "It wouldn't be good for someone to walk in on two demons fighting in a church."

"You think just because I'm a kid that I can't take you?" Christian shouted, coming at him again.

Christian resembled a small version of Louis as a demon. The transformation made him powerful looking, his wide expansive wings pulsating with the rage he felt.

"Wait! Hold on! You have nothing to prove to me." Louis shouted, holding out his hands. "I don't even know who you are, and I don't want to fight you. I just want to understand what's going. I came here for information more than anything else," he said, hoping the lie would mask his true intentions long enough for him to come up with a way to subdue him somehow.

"Well, I know who you are, Louis." He said with a snicker. "As for me, my name's Christian."

"Really?" Louis said sarcastically. "A half breed demon named 'Christian'? What is it with parents and odd names these days?"

"Your humor only shows how weak your human side has made you. I am the last child of Lilith. I am more than just a half breed." Christian growled angrily.

"Yeah, I could tell. When I first saw your handy work I wondered why I'd never heard of you before, but I imagine you travel a lot." Louis said, hoping to keep Christian talking. "And I suppose the 'Lilith' you mentioned is none other than the first woman, the one thrown out of Paradise?"

"Of course, there's none other like her, my mother." He replied balling his hands into fists. "She's the most powerful woman of all."

"I'm sure every kid thinks that about their mother, but getting back to the information I need. Why are you killing people? I can understand the foster parents, because you've probably been doing that for a long time, but a dirty priest, one that liked young boys?" He shook his head and gestured at him with his hands. "I would think what he was doing would make him more valuable alive."

"I have my reasons." Christian spat.

"Okay, fair enough. I guess since you know me you've probably met my brother?" Louis asked expectantly.

"I'd heard you were a detective." Christian flashed him an evil smile, "But you're not going to interrogate me any further. I won't allow it."

"Like I said, I just want information." Louis repeated.

"You mean, like about your girlfriend?" Christian scoffed, reaching into the pocket of his jeans. They had been nearly shredded by his transformation, but his pocket was still intact, as was the small mirror he pulled out. "I put her in here! If you want her so bad, here, take her!" He threw the mirror at him.

Louis was confused, he had no idea what the demon was talking about, but he caught the mirror before it could hit the floor and possibly shatter. He chanced a quick look at it and saw Elizabeth in the mirror.

"What the fuck?" He shouted to Christian. "I didn't even know she was still alive."

"Apparently there's a lot going on that you don't know about." Christian kicked off the floor and hovered close to Louis. "Now can we cut through all the bullshit and get on with things?" He swiped at Louis, long claws grazing the side of his face, leaving streaks of blood.

Louis cried out in agony as fiery pain exploded on the side of his face. He clutched at the slashes in anger, feeling the lacerations, jagged flesh in his fingers. *"If he got me a little lower I'd have my throat torn open."* He looked down at the blood on his hands and felt the rage explode inside him with every throb of the wound.

"I wanted information, I didn't want this! I didn't want to fight unless I had to, remember that!" Louis shouted to Christian. He felt the darkness rising up, he wanted to fight it, wanted to refuse accepting it. Christian swiped at him again, opening a long deep gash in his forearm, which he'd held up defensively. By then it was too late to fight it, he just let happen, his body growing, bones stretching and popping, skin splitting open. He was becoming a demon again, but under the circumstances he reveled in it rather than despised it. That wasn't an emotion he was comfortable with, but he knew deep down he had no choice but to change.

Christian dove past him again, claws ready for another swipe, but in spite of being in mid-transformation Louis grabbed him by the throat and slammed him into the floor. The demon-boy lay sprawled out, winded and stunned when Louis went to work on his hands.

Grabbing each of his hands in his own, Louis squeezed with all his strength until he felt the bones crack and break, then he slammed each hand into the floor.

"You wanna fuckin' claw someone like a little girl?" He roared furiously, "Try it now! Unlike your usual helpless victim I fight back, and no two-bit punk with claws and wings is going to get the better of me!"

Louis grabbed a bowl of holy water off of a pedestal and threw it at Christian. His skin sizzled and burned as the water splashed on it.

"I see whose side you're ultimately on now," Louis shouted, his own hands wet from the blessed water, but since he still had faith, his flesh didn't burn. "That'll make what I'm about to do a lot easier on my conscience!"

He shrugged out of what remained of his human skin, eyes glowing blood-red.

Christian struggled to stand, screaming at the agony in his hands, but he didn't give up. He lunged at Louis, trying to form his hands into warped looking fists to punch him with, but Louis was both too fast and too powerful for him. He laced his fingers together and simply hit Christian as hard as he could with both hands, hammering him into the air toward the ceiling. Then, kicking off the floor, he soared high to hit him yet again in midair, knocking him through a window of the church, shattering the stained glass.

"That miserable little bastard!" Louis shouted enraged. He cursed to himself when he realized that by sending Christian through a window he'd unintentionally allowed him to escape. Louis leapt into the air, set on trying to catch up and subdue him, but then he saw the mirror lying on the floor across the room. He raced to it, allowing time to resume and willing himself to become human once again along the way.

When his feet touched the ground Louis stared into the mirror, watching Elizabeth pound her fists on the other side of the glass, looking like she was shouting. His face, the wounds beginning to painfully heal as he returned to his human form, still dripped blood. Some of it landed in a red smear on the dark glass.

Suddenly the mirror hissed and sputtered, then exploded, sending Louis sprawling several feet away.

When the smoke cleared seconds later, Elizabeth was there, lying on the floor coughing and struggling to stand. Just then, Tindilli burst into the church, his sidearm out and pointing forward protectively.

"Louis?" He called out. "Where the hell are you?" His eyes darted around and searched in every direction as he carefully made his way down the center aisle of the church. He headed toward the back of the room, where he saw a shattered window and what looked like the body of a woman lying on the floor in front of the altar. He felt more at ease when he heard her coughing. *"At least she's still alive, whoever it is."* He thought, relieved that he didn't have to call a coroner just yet.

"I'm over here," Louis said, pushing himself up from the floor. He shook his head to clear it, the ringing in his ears causing him to stagger and clutch at his forehead. He heard coughing, and swung his head up to see Elizabeth on the floor across the room from him.

Shrugging off the pain, he raced to her side, seeing Tindilli come up on them out of the corner of his eye.

"Elizabeth!" Louis said, turning her over. His eyes widened when he saw her face, looking just as it was the last time he'd seen her in the cemetery when they both fought his father, right before she 'died'.

Her breathing was harsh and raspy, but when he whispered her name again and lightly tapped her on the cheek her eyes fluttered open. She stared at Louis for a moment before clutching onto him, hugging him so hard his ribs ached and the wounds on his face throbbed when they rubbed against her.

"Oh Louis, you shouldn't have let him escape!" She pulled away to look him in the eye. "I was trying to tell you that from inside the mirror. I was shouting as loudly as I could."

"To hell with that right now!" Louis said annoyed. "How is it that you're still alive? I watched you die."

"Never mind that, we've got to get that kid!" Elizabeth urged. "He's going to keep killing! We've got to stop him!"

"Can one of you tell me what's going on here?" Tindilli asked angrily. "Do I need to call for an ambulance or back-up?"

"I think we're both okay." Louis said, helping Elizabeth to her feet.

"What happened?" Tindilli asked. "Where's the kid?"

"Well, it's a long story, and I didn't plan it to go down like this, but I screwed up, he got away." Louis said, sounding as disappointed as the expression on his face.

"And who exactly are you?" Tindilli demanded, frustrated by what Louis had just told him.

"I'm Elizabeth, Elizabeth Duffy." She said, looking at him curiously.

"Oh, I've heard a lot about you, but I thought you were supposed to be dead." He said, at a loss.

"That's also a long story." She said with a tight grin. "Up until a few minutes ago I was trapped in a cursed mirror. A few drops of

Louis' blood gave me an extra boost of strength and I was able to break free."

"That's great, but now there are two long stories I'd better be hearing, like now." Tindilli said, shaking his head. "I need answers."

"We really don't have time for this," Elizabeth insisted. "We've got to see if we can pick up the boy's trail."

"He's not going to get far in the condition he was in, at least not for a while. I messed him up pretty bad." Louis assured her. "We'll find him one way or another." He saw some scraps of Christian's shirt lying on the floor spattered with blood. "I can probably use this later to find him. We'll work it out. He's not going to be roaming free for long."

"What about the church?" Tindilli gestured around to the blood and other debris. "We've got to get this place cleaned up before someone comes up here and starts asking questions."

"The skin we shed is already starting to turn to dust," Louis pointed out. "There's nothing much else to clean up." Louis looked around the inside of the church. Other than the window, there wasn't much damage done by the fight or the explosion.

"I can't fix the window," Louis said to Elizabeth. "Can you?"

She nodded. With a wave of her hands the glass swirled up from the floor and reformed in the window frame looking as good as new.

"What's going on in here?" Father Volip said, coming out of his office, rubbing the side of his head. "Where's Christian?"

"The kid knocked him out before we fought," Louis whispered to Tindilli. He cast an illusion around himself so his clothes would look just as they had when he arrived, and not torn up and tattered from his transformation. Tindilli stepped back and did a double-take for a moment before realizing what he did.

The priest came around the side of the altar, looked at Louis, and then saw Elizabeth and Tindilli standing there.

"Who are they?" He asked, confused.

"They're my partners." Louis said, reluctantly lying in order to avoid explaining everything that just transpired. "We needed to take Christian into custody for questioning regarding several recent crimes, but when he found out why we wanted him he escaped."

"Yes," Tindilli cut in, "If you see or hear anything about him please give us a call as soon as possible." He handed the priest a business card. "It's really important that we get him off the streets as soon as possible. There may be lives at stake."

"We'd better get going." Louis said to Volip, "It's been a long day and we need to get back to the station."

"Okay," Father Volip said looking lost and squinting at the card.

"You're lucky I didn't call for back-up before I got here." Tindilli mumbled while they walked out of the church. "That would have been a fiasco."

"At least we really know what we're dealing with now." Louis sounded relieved.

"No, 'we' don't." Tindilli stopped in his tracks and looked at both of them. "You two need to tell me what's going on, and I mean now. I can't be in the middle of this and not know what's happening."

"Okay, let's go to my place, it's not that far from here," Louis said. "We can all spill our guts there over coffee. And please, remind me to pick up my car when we're done talking. It's still in New Jersey."

EIGHT

Daniel woke to the first rays of the sun shining through his bedroom window. Feeling the warmth on his face reminded him why he got a suite on the east side of the building. Mornings were always a stunning sight to behold. He turned his head toward the bright light and saw the nude silhouette of her standing next to the window, slowly drawing the drapes closed.

Lilith.

She was breathtakingly beautiful. He was amazed at how, even shrouded in the shadows he could make out her body's every perfect line and curve. He vividly remembered the feeling of having her against him, of being engulfed by her. Daniel was lost in it all like an endless maze, her scent, her touch, everything about her. He couldn't even describe what he felt with words, it was too new and overwhelming.

From the time he'd spent at the bar with her the previous evening, to that morning, he learned many forms of passion and his life had changed yet again. It was a drastic change indeed, because there were so many things his mind and heart still had to process, so many things he had to figure out, and though it was overpowering, none of it really seemed to matter anymore.

Daniel was happy, happier then he'd ever been in his entire life, and part of it was because he'd met a woman, and it wasn't just any woman, it was the first one ever created. It was also the first living human to be cast out of paradise, rejected just as he had been since birth.

"She's like a goddess," he thought, *"an amazing woman, and she picked me of all people to be with!"*

It was that thought that stayed with him because it set him apart from everyone else. For the first time being singled out was a good thing.

Daniel had never experienced affection

from a woman before, not ever in his life, not even as a child. Lilith had introduced him to it as an adult, and as a man. It wasn't just the sex, the insanely animalistic and powerful sex that he had just learned about; it was everything that led up to it and went along with it afterward. She spoke to him tenderly, as a man, an equal and as if she really cared. When Lilith touched him, whether it was the brush of her lips on his cheek or simply just holding his hand, he knew bliss, a sort of heaven that he never expected could exist.

"Good morning Daniel," she whispered to him, her voice low and throaty. "Why don't we sleep in today, at least for an hour or so? After last night we can both probably use the rest." She giggled in a way that seemed very uncharacteristic and nearly childlike, then slowly climbed on the bed to straddle him.

"By all means," he sighed happily, sitting up to wrap his arms around her, "sleeping in sounds wonderful!" He pulled her down on top of him.

****

By the time they slept, Daniel was exhausted.

The nightmares came out of nowhere.

He was in his demon form somewhere in Hell. The image of his surroundings was so vivid, so real, that he thought he could smell the rotting flesh of sinners and the acrid scent of sulfur in the air. He didn't recognize the cavern that he stood in, or the deep pit alongside it. What he did recognize was himself, or at least a different side of himself, and when he saw it his heart raced with panic and fear.

Stuck to the eerily glowing stone wall facing him was his human form; an empty body of flesh, hanging like a sack on two metal spikes that had been pounded into the stonewall. He looked down at his hands. They were still dark and scaly, and his claws were at his fingertips, as sharp as ever. He squeezed his eyes shut to block everything around him out in an attempt to transform into his human self.

Nothing happened.

"Why can't I change back?" He whispered to himself, angry and upset. "This doesn't make sense! I'm whole now! I don't have to look like this!"

"Whole?" The word echoed loudly around Daniel, and he immediately recognized the raspy voice, a chill climbing up his spine.

B'lial burst up from the floor of the cavern right in front of Daniel. He hovered there for a moment, scowling at him, and then he reached out, grabbed Daniel by the throat. With a burst of speed, he flew toward the back wall where he pinned his son high up, holding him there by his throat.

Daniel could only hang there, arms and legs flailing, barely able to breathe. There was no way for him to get free. B'lial was too strong for him alone.

"You're not whole you bastard! You're a parody of both a demon and a man!" He shouted in his face. "There's a piece of me raging there inside you and I'll have it back before you know it!"

B'lial pulled away from the wall, still clutching Daniel by the throat, carrying him over the pit. The pit itself darkened to an inky blackness, a void that swirled around like a tornado. Daniel felt the force of it tugging at him.

"Go home you useless sack!" B'lial shouted, tossing him into the void.

Daniel woke in a cold sweat, his arms flailing, feet kicking as if he were actually falling. B'lial's final words still rang in his ears. When he pulled himself together a moment later he took a deep breath and covered his face in his hands.

"That was crazy!" He flipped over in bed, reaching for Lilith, but he found that she wasn't there beside him. "Lilith?"

"Where is she?" He wondered frantically, but then his train of thought changed. *"Was she ever really here or did I imagine all of it? Was it one of my own illusions working against me somehow? Maybe it's B'lial's way of getting*

revenge for his defeat?"

At first he honestly thought he might have been losing his mind, especially after the nightmare, but then he heard the shower running in the bathroom, saw a cloud of steam filling the doorway, and his heart slowed.

"I guess I'm not as crazy as I thought I was." He thought to himself, grateful.

"I thought I'd freshen up a bit with a nice hot shower." Lilith said, standing nude in the doorway. "Would you care to join me? I'll wash your back if you wash mine." Her eyes lit up and she licked her lips at him.

Daniel immediately forgot his nightmare along with the words B'lial taunted him with. He could only see, only focus on, the beautiful woman in the doorway and the way the light caressed her flawless skin and the toned muscles underneath it. He felt drunk, but knew he hadn't had a drink since he left the bar. *"I feel like I can devour her. I want to. Is this what it feels like to be in love?"* He thought to himself. *"Am I in love, lust, or just going insane?"*

Without giving it any further thought, he swept off the sheet that covered him, swung his legs out of the bed and grabbed Lilith, kissing her hard on the mouth, pressing her whole body against him.

"You don't have to ask me twice." He whispered in her ear, wrapping an arm around her, guiding her to the shower.

****

Over an hour later they were finally dressing trying to decide where to eat dinner.

"Maybe we should just have room service send us something up again." Lilith smiled, slipping into a black and gray dress she'd had delivered to the hotel from a shop down the block. "The food here is fantastic and it's always fun to eat in bed."

"That it is," Daniel said, blushing slightly as he buttoned his shirt. "I think we should get out a little though, see the sights of Fall in the city and find somewhere cozy to eat. We've got all the time in the world to spend together."

"You know, you're nothing at all like what I expected when I first saw you sitting there, looking so handsome in that dark suit." She shook her head and looked at him sideways. "I expected to find a very angry, bitter demon ready to take on the world for screwing him so badly for as long as it had. How is it you're so 'nice'? You're a demon with a bad past. I don't understand."

"I was born who I am," he said sighing. "It's not the fault of the world that I came into it this way. It's certainly not how I would have had it if the choice had been given to me; but furiously killing people and destroying things, looking for vengeance? It may have given me a slight taste of satisfaction but it could never make me happy when all was said and done."

"But even the room; you paid for it in cash, real money. Where'd you get it from?" She asked expectantly. "You couldn't have had that kind of money lying around."

Daniel wasn't sure if he should tell her about Hell, Dantalians' pit and how he could travel between there and earth. He didn't know how much she knew about him and didn't want to screw things up.

"I took it from Hell, my other home." He said, throwing caution to the wind. "With my father gone, everything that was his is now mine. I have a place in Hell complete with minions and money."

"You took money out of Hell?" Lilith sounded shocked. "You shouldn't be doing that. Everything that goes to Hell is supposed to stay there. Yes, your father had a domain and minions, but they weren't just his, they were also the Master's. Everything is ultimately the Master's unless he says so. We all belong to him in one way or another, and we all have a job to do. I tempt people. I give them a reason to be wicked, and I enjoy doing it. I can get right into a persons' head and know what makes them tick, good or bad. Oh, there are so many things I can do, as if you didn't already know about some of them."

Daniel felt confused. He'd never actually

met the Master, he was just glad to have been able to finally find a place in Hell, to know his dark side. He had no idea what was expected of him, what his 'job' was supposed to be.

"What am I supposed to do, learn how to be as evil as my father? B'lial, you should have taught me more than resentment and indifference, and then maybe I would've known more than sadness." Daniel thought to himself bitterly.

"Your father never explained anything about this to you, did he?" Frustrated and disappointed, Lilith could only shake her head. She pulled Daniel down to sit beside her on the bed. "This is all too strange. There's a lot you need to know about, more than I thought."

"My father told me that since I wasn't 'right' like my brother Louis, the Master didn't want any part of me in Hell. With the way I looked before, no one wanted me around on earth either." He said, bewildered. "He simply disowned me. He'd drop by to look in on me every once in a while, but up until a year ago when he wanted me to help him 'turn' Louis, I was basically useless to him. When Louis and I finally defeated him in Hell, I was able to take the darkness from him. I thought I was free to live on earth and Hell as I pleased. That's what he did. I made a real identity for myself here and now I can go back and forth whenever I want to. It would be the closest thing I could have to a normal life." He looked at her sincerely, "Ever since I was a kid, that's all I ever wanted."

"You're right; you can live in both worlds, and if the Master was against what you're doing you'd already know it, but there's more to it than that." She looked into his eyes. "Everything your father had is yours, but you have to understand that he did things to maintain what was his. You'll have to maintain it all as well if you expect to have that normal life you crave so much."

"What do you mean, 'maintain'?" Daniel was confused. "And how is it you know so much about Hell?"

"Um, because I was there when it was just created," she said sarcastically. "I remember it when it was empty, when things were just starting to get interesting."

"I'm sorry, I don't mean to sound so ignorant, but this is all still very new to me, especially anything having to do with B'lial." Daniel felt foolish, but wanted to learn as much as possible so he didn't lose what he had. "Please, by all means tell me more. I need to know more about things if I want to survive in both worlds."

"Souls are like currency, sort of like Hell's cash. You can essentially 'buy' anything in Hell by acquiring souls. The more you have the better. You upset the balance by taking things out of Hell. You're going to have to replace what you took."

Daniel thought about it for a second and realized what she was saying made sense, but it was also terrible, because he had no way to return what he'd taken. *"I'll figure something out."*

"Souls are something Hell always needs, and chaos in any way shape or form means power. If you make people sin that gets you more power." Lilith said casually. "That's why I was surprised you're so 'nice'. You need to turn souls from the light to the dark, or at least kill some people. You see, there's no way to be a good person in Hell, and there's no escape from being there either. You'd be challenged by other demons constantly, demons that envy your position and want it for themselves. Envy, jealousy, they're really powerful sins. Unless you want to end up like your father you've got some work to do."

Daniel sat there looking into her eyes, quiet determination beginning to grow.

"I just want to live for once, actually enjoy it too and not have people be afraid of me." He put his head down, "Why do I have to go through this now? I thought things were finally going to be great. I was welcome in Hell and I'd never have to live on the streets again." He pounded a fist into the bed.

"There's a lot more to existence then what you're talking about, and everything has a price no matter how big or how small." She stood up and looked down at him. "It sounds like you want to live in a fairy tale and that's impossible. You're going to have to start paying the price yourself for everything you've got and everything you desire."

Daniel reluctantly nodded.

"I always lived life doing what I had to do in order to survive. Sometimes I had to do things-" He let his words trail off, then grimly looked up into Lilith's eyes. "I'd hoped to live my life differently now, but I will do whatever I have to, no matter what."

Lilith's expression softened and she caressed his face in her hands.

"We can get started at dinner." She kissed him on the forehead, and then spoke quickly. "Let's go somewhere really nice where we can fuck with people's lives without them even knowing. It'll make dinner go down exquisitely."

NINE

Before heading to Louis' brownstone, the three of them searched around the church, easily finding the spot on the ground where Christian landed after being thrown out the window. There was blood on the grass and a slight indentation in the ground.

"There are no footprints leading away from here so he must have been well enough to fly off." Louis said. He looked at Elizabeth. "I don't sense him anywhere, do you?"

She shook her head.

"Well, let's get out of here before anyone comes outside and starts asking questions. The less we have to answer for, the less I have to cover up later." Tindilli said. "My car is out front, I'll drive if you don't mind." He said, not wanting Louis to even suggest traveling via his shadow. He hadn't done it a lot, but it was far from a pleasant experience for him.

It was late by the time they got to the brownstone. Louis brought them inside where he was immediately greeted by Bruce, who cackled and screeched at him for being away for so long without letting him know what was going on.

"I know Bruce but I had work to do." He let the illusion he'd cast over his appearance fade. "See? It was a rough night, I've got to go up and change."

Louis left Tindilli and Elizabeth in the living room with Bruce while he ran upstairs to change into some fresh clothes. When he came back down clad in a tank top and jeans a few minutes later he brought them into the kitchen where they sat around the table while Louis put on a pot of coffee. "You know John Tindilli already, but you've never really met Elizabeth." He gestured to her. "Apparently, she's not dead like we all thought."

Elizabeth caught the sarcasm in his tone and smirked at him.

"Now before we get into anything about the kid, I want to know why you tricked me into thinking that you were dead." Louis turned away from the counter and pointed at her. "That was a really fucked up thing to do to me."

"I was worried that if B'lial or any of his minions knew I was alive after the incident in the cemetery that they'd use me against you." She said flatly. "I couldn't take the risk. I would have come to you eventually when I knew things were safe again."

"Your store wasn't even real!" Louis ranted, his eyes momentarily turning bright red.

Bruce took that as his cue to leap off the table and fly upstairs.

"I didn't know you and your brother destroyed B'lial. If I did I would have come here in a heartbeat to set the record straight." She said defensively.

Louis opened his mouth to say something but Tindilli beat him to the punch, shoving his hand up in front of his face in a halting gesture.

"Look, I know you two have something going on, but Louis, now that you know why she did what she did let's get on to Christian and the murders. You two can talk details later."

Louis let himself calm down. He got coffee for everyone and then sat down at the table and lit a cigarette.

"So Christian told me that his mother is Lilith, and that he's helping her with

something by committing the murders."
Elizabeth said. "I couldn't get him to tell me
anything more before getting taken off guard.
He was quick, caught me off guard and
trapped me. That's why I was stuck in the
mirror when you found me."

"Who's Lilith?" Tindilli said, confused.
"You made it sound like she's important in all
this. Is she like the mother in that old Cagney
movie 'White Heat'?"

"Sort of." Louis said after thinking about it
for a moment. "Lilith is the first woman,
created before Eve."

"What?" Tindilli's eyes widened.

"I know, it's not exactly common
knowledge, but Eve wasn't the first woman."
Louis went on. "She was created just like
Adam, from the earth, but she refused to be
subjected to Adam's domination, especially
during sex. She thought of herself as his equal
and wouldn't even allow him to get on top of
her."

"Do I really need to know all this?"
Tindilli asked, annoyed.

"Well, knowledge is power, especially
when dealing with demons." Elizabeth
chimed in.

"Anyway, she was thrown out of Paradise,
Eden, and then Eve was created." Louis
stopped to gulp down some coffee. "If I get
any of this wrong correct me." He said to

Elizabeth. "After being banished from Paradise, she roamed around aimlessly until she was found by demons."

"B'lial was one of them." Elizabeth cut in again. "That's why she knows him and in turn knows who you and your brother are."

"Lilith had babies, lots of babies over the centuries," Louis smirked at her and continued on, "and they were like me, half demon, but they're different too, because Lilith wasn't just human, she'd been corrupted by the demons she'd taken up with. The kid that's murdering people, Christian; he's her last child."

"Okay, I got it." Tindilli said, puffing on a fresh cigar. "Now what if B'lial was the person she was doing a favor for?"

"That could be, but B'lial's gone, isn't he?" Louis looked at Elizabeth. "Obscure ripped B'lial's heart out and stole some of his darkness, just enough to make him whole, more like me."

"You mean your brother has a piece of B'lial inside him?" Elizabeth's eyes narrowed at him. "That's insane! He should never have done that. He must be so screwed up right now, having a piece of true demon inside him."

"But B'lial was already beaten, and by the time Bruce and I got thrown back here his body was already starting to turn to dust."

"Yes, but demons don't ever really die.

They're just reduced to spiritual matter and then reside in the lowest pit of Hell until the Master raises them again, if he ever does." Elizabeth explained. "That small bit of B'lial that he absorbed is still B'lial. Unlike an organ transplant or something, his identity is still in what was taken. Over time it could get stronger, influencing him."

"Okay," Tindilli said, holding both of his hands up at them. "So let me get this straight. We have a kid that's part demon, and he's killing people to help his mother, Lilith, who's the first real woman and also an old friend of B'lial's. She's using her son's help to follow through with a favor she owes someone. In the meantime, your brother, who is also half demon, took part of B'lial inside himself so he could be more like you." He knocked the ashes off his cigar and squinted at Louis. "Sure, that all makes sense, right?" Tindilli chuckled. "Seriously, we've got it all right there, even if the favor isn't for B'lial. The kid's murdering for his mother. We have to get him off the streets as soon as possible. Maybe we can track him down and get both of them?"

"Then after the dust settles we can find out exactly what this 'favor' is and who it's for from Lilith." Elizabeth added.

"Yeah, but there's a bigger picture here too." Louis said. "If my brother is being affected by B'lial he could very well be involved with all this. I've got find him and see if I can talk him into getting rid of that part of B'lial that he stole."

"Let's find the kid, what was his name, Christian, first before anyone else gets killed." Tindilli gnawed on his cigar. "We don't need any more bodies piling up."

"Okay, but once I locate him I've got to track down my brother too." Louis mashed out his cigarette and pulled the tattered piece of Christian's shirt from of his back pocket and tossed it on the table. "Then I'm going to have to send a tow truck to go get my car back in New Jersey, because there's no way I'm going to be able to pick it up anytime soon."

Bruce suddenly flew into the room, dropping a sheet of paper on the table in front of Louis. He read it aloud when the raven landed in front of the only other empty seat.

STILL NO FOOD

PIZZA

"We never did get a chance to go grocery shopping, I'm sorry Bruce. You must be so hungry." Louis looked at Tindilli and Elizabeth. "Are you guys up for some take-out while I locate Christian?"

****

Christian saw Louis swing at him. He moved so quickly that there was no way to avoid getting hit. Bright lights flashed in the back of his head when his opponent's fists slammed into him. He crashed through the window of the church in agony and hit the ground hard. He tried to cushion the fall, and thrust his hands out instinctively, but the act of moving them brought fiery pain. He attempted to flip his wings up too, in order to slow his fall to a glide, but his hands hurt so much he couldn't think straight anymore. He knew he had a few broken ribs on top of it all, having coughed up blood when he tried to take a deep breath while he was on the ground.

"I never got hit so hard before in my life, and that's saying a lot. Considering how old I really am." He mumbled, feeling around the inside of his mouth with his tongue. "I think that son of a bitch knocked out two of my teeth!"

He got to his feet and stumbled on unsteady legs, then leaped into the air. His wings swung down powerfully and he was airborne.

"All I have to do is get far enough away!" He thought, *"I can't let him find me!"*

He was weak, too weak to continue on in the air for much longer. His mind raced, trying to think of a safe place to hide, but he couldn't think of anywhere. He couldn't even go home to his dead foster parent's house because the police had it under surveillance. He could only think of one thing to do.

"Lily,' he mumbled."I've got to find my

mother! She can help me; give me a place to stay until I'm all healed up." He let his senses fan out gradually but the pain in his side, the broken ribs moving around, hurt too much for him to stay airborne. Each time he moved his wings it felt as if he was getting stabbed in his side. He landed roughly on the roof of an old building, twisting his right ankle when his feet touched the ground.

"Damn it!" he shouted, limping over to lean on the door to the stairway. His breathing had become a wheezing sound and he coughed up blood again. The pain was too much for him, he turned back into a human boy that looked like he'd been hit by a freight train.

The weathered old door on the roof was locked, but even in his weakened state he was able to push his way though it and stumble down the stairs. The building had five floors and the elevator wasn't in operation, so he slowly made his way to the ground floor, stopping several times to rest. He was careful to avoid anyone on his way down, but he followed his senses, listening carefully.

Christian knew being seen would be a problem. He was much too weak to cast an illusion to alter his appearance, and he looked terrible. His shirt was torn to shreds by his transformation and his pants were barely hanging on. *"At least I didn't lose my sneakers."* He thought, *"Not that it helped to prevent me from hurting my ankle."*

By the time he reached the ground floor it was a struggle just staying upright, but there was nothing he could do to help himself, nowhere to even sit down and catch his breath.

"How am I going to get out of here much less find Lily?" His answer came a moment later when he heard a man leaving his apartment in a rush. He heard the man mumbling curses about being late, and peeked through the narrow rectangular window in the door he was hidden behind and watched what apartment he came out of.

"Bingo!" he whispered.

Christian quietly crept into the hallway, listening for anyone that might be roaming around or leaving the other apartments. There were three doors in the hall besides the one he headed to. It was easy to keep an eye on them as he tried the lock on the door.

He wasn't surprised to find that the door was locked, but in his haste the man didn't lock the deadbolt, only the doorknob, which Christian found easy to push in.

When he was safely inside, he closed and locked the door behind him using the deadbolt. It was a small one bedroom apartment, with a tiny kitchen and a bathroom that only had a shower stall.

Christian removed what was left of his shirt and tossed it on the floor. Then he ran the water in the sink so that it would be hot and grabbed a towel, which he tore into three long strips. He used one to clean himself off with and the other two to wrap his wounds. It was difficult and very painful to wrap his ribs but he managed to make it tight enough so he could stand upright. Wrapping his ankle was easier, but he couldn't tie the laces on his sneaker.

The pain in his ankle wasn't too bad if he allowed himself to limp, but his ribs still hurt like fire under his skin and he was lucky to be able to stand.

"This guy must be the only person on the planet without any painkillers or prescription drugs in his medicine cabinet." He cursed to himself, feeling light headed. *"I was really hoping for a few painkillers or at the very least, some aspirin."*

He walked in the sole bedroom and couldn't help but laugh. It was full of sports memorabilia. There was so much inside that there was barely enough room for the bed. Signed posters, framed and immaculate, hung from the walls, and there were two cabinets with everything from sports cards to signed baseballs and basketballs on display inside. He rummaged through the man's drawers and managed to find a tank top small enough to wear. It was very long, but that was a good thing because Christian's pants were filthy and a little torn. Looking in the tiny closet, he flipped a baseball hat onto his head and grabbed a gray sweatshirt. It covered him well. He rolled up the sleeves and began searching around for money.

"It figures that there's no cash lying around." He mused. *"All this signed crap probably sends him to the poorhouse every month."*

He did manage to find a change jar, but there wasn't much in it. He pocketed a couple of dollars and moved on. Christian wasn't surprised to see that there wasn't much to eat in the fridge, and didn't even bother trying to see if anything was edible, he just closed the door decided it was time to leave.

Not wanting to leave any blatant evidence behind, Christian grabbed his shirt from the bathroom floor and headed out the door. He'd find a place to ditch his shirt in his travels.

The pain wasn't as intense as it was earlier, but he knew over time, with having to walk upright, that he'd be in agony soon enough. He still had to locate Lily, and hope that when he did find her he could use public transportation to reach her.

"It'll be easier to sense where she is when I'm out in the open." He said, *"She's not going to be too happy about what happened."*

TEN

"So how exactly is having that scrap of his shirt going to help us find him?" Tindilli asked when they moved to the living room. "Are you hiding a half demon bloodhound somewhere?"

"Ha, ha, ha," Louis clapped his hands, annoyed. "You hear that Elizabeth? He made a funny."

"Yeah, real funny." She grinned at him. "Louis and I are going to try to channel our power and use it to pinpoint where Christian is in the city. He's a lot more difficult to find because we've never dealt with him or anyone like him before. Having his mother's blood makes him a natural at hiding."

"Yeah, and being in here should be a little more relaxing." Louis said, unfolding a map of the city on the coffee table.

Elizabeth sat on the couch facing the windows. It was black leather, and looked very dusty. "You know, I never saw the inside of your brownstone before Louis." She wiped her hand on the top of the couch, then pointed it at him so he could see all the dirt on her hand. "You may want to get a cleaning lady if you can't find enough time to dust."

"Oh you're a riot too," Louis snickered, pulling over a leather recliner from the corner of the room. "C'mon, let's get this going already."

Louis sat in the chair directly across from Elizabeth with the map between them. He tore a thin strip from the scrap of shirt and tied it around a yellow highlighter.

"I think this should work just fine." He said, holding out his hand for Elizabeth. "I've never done this before, so you're going to have to walk me through it. Whenever I had to find anyone I just always use my shadow."

"No problem. Just concentrate Louis, put everything out of your mind and just focus on Christian." She leaned forward and put her hand around his. "If you have to, close your eyes and just let yourself go."

"Looks like you're using a low budget Ouija board." Tindilli mumbled under his breath. "I just hope this works."

Bruce flew into the room and sat on top of the couch next to him, watching Louis and Elizabeth move the highlighter around on the map.

"I think it's safe to say he's moving around a lot." Tindilli said to Bruce, watching how the highlighter moved around the map. He leaned back on the couch and gnawed on his cigar, tapping his fingers nervously.

When the highlighter finally stopped moving Elizabeth let go of Louis' hand and sat back. She looked at the map and grinned.

"So where are we going?" Louis looked at the yellow mark. "Ah, it looks like an old warehouse in Hell's Kitchen. We can get there really quick if you don't mind going through my shadow." He looked at Tindilli, who was reluctant to do it before.

"I don't want to, but the clock says way after midnight and if I don't get home soon Cindy will have my head." Tindilli laughed. "I don't think I have a choice, so do your thing so we can get this over with."

"Well then let's go." Louis said standing up. "The sooner we get this over with the sooner I can get to my brother, not that I want to visit Hell, but I have to." He willed his shadow to spread out, and the far wall was suddenly covered in blackness, like a starless night. He took both their hands and guided them through the darkness.

They walked into the chilly night with the sprawling warehouse in front of them. None of them knew what to expect.

"I'll take point, you guys back me up." Tindilli took out his gun and pointed it at the ground, stepping forward toward the old abandoned building.

"Is he crazy?" Elizabeth looked at Louis with a confused look on her face.

"He's my mentor, and there's no one else I'd want in my corner." Louis said following close behind.

The inside of the warehouse was essentially empty except for some old broken down equipment and a lot of trash. Louis could sense the rats, and there were a lot of them, but they didn't want to be bothered. There were more than enough bugs and street trash to eat at any given time of the day.

"Wait a minute Tindilli," Louis took a step back and a deep breath. "Just hold on." He pulled out a piece of the fabric that they had tied around the highlighter and sniffed it.

"What's going on?" Tindilli asked, his sidearm still out.

"I think we've got him." He replied, seeing a dumpster nearby. Louis pointed to it and nodded. "I'm going in." He whispered, heading in that direction.

The three of them fanned out around the dumpster with Louis in the center. He counted down with his fingers so the others could see and then with a nod he leaped on top of it and flipped open the lid. His expression abruptly changed to disappointment, and he jumped down inside it.

A moment later he climbed out with what was left of Christian's shirt.

"Well, back to square one." Tindilli holstered his revolver.

"Not necessarily." Louis said. "I think we should head back. I'll send Bruce out to look for him. He can get his scent from the shirt. While he's doing that I'm going to pay my brother a visit, see if having a piece of B'lial inside him has driven him crazy yet. Maybe he can give us a lead on things."

****

They had dinner at Masseria Dei Vini, an Italian Restaurant. Daniel was grateful that Lilith knew how to read Italian, because he wouldn't have been able to order otherwise. She ordered so many appetizers that he wondered if he'd still be able to eat a meal.

"The Italians have always known how to eat," Lilith said, eating veal raviolis. "I ordered us duck for dinner, I hope you don't mind. It's exceptionally good."

"Not at all," Daniel smiled at her and tried

not to act too shy in the restaurant. "I have to thank you for bringing me here. I would have settled for a walk around the Hudson and a sandwich, but this, well, I'm really enjoying it." He'd never been to a place like it before, and the food was also very new to him. Everything was so rich tasting and wonderful. The only things he'd ever eaten that he considered Italian food before was stale pizza and pasta from an outdated can.

"Daniel, do you see that man over there in the dark blue suit?" Lilith asked. "When you look over there try to do it nonchalantly."

He turned his head slightly and saw the man she was referring to out of the corner of his eye. "Yes, I see him."

"We can start with him." Lilith chuckled, eyes lit up wickedly. "He's really got a lot of shit going on. Being married with a kid isn't enough; he's also got a girl on the side that's half his age that his wife doesn't know about. She's pregnant too."

"How do you know this?" He asked, looking at her strangely.

"Who do you think set him up with his girlfriend?" She grinned.

"You know a lot about people doing bad things." Daniel said flatly.

"I am the first true sinner, so I know a sin when I see it." Lilith said casually. "There are so many good sins in this restaurant right now.

If we wanted to we could really have a riot going on in a very short time."

"What do you want to do?" Daniel asked.

"I tell ya what; we'll do the easy one to start with." She smiled. "That guy's got a cell phone sitting out on their table. There's a number in it for his girlfriend. If you can make his phone ring with her number I'll do the rest."

"Okay, I'll try. What's the girls' name?" He asked, focusing on the phone sitting on the side of the table.

"Her name's Sophia. But you better hurry, the waiter is coming." She urged.

Daniel focused his mind on the phone. When he could see it clearly he found the name and number he was looking for.

"I haven't used this ability very much; it's a new one I picked up from my father, so if I slip up I apologize ahead of time." He said, still not completely comfortable with being able to do things using his mind.

The phone was clear in his mind. He held out a hand as if it were resting in it, then pressed the button with his index finger.

The man's phone suddenly rang. He picked it up to answer, and just as he was about to put the phone to his ear, a waiter passing by the table carrying a tray of pasta tripped up and dropped a plate all over the man. He didn't even see it coming, and tossed his phone in the air, not realizing until it was too late that the phone was going to land directly in front of his wife.

The waiter fell to one knee, able to hang onto everything else except for the plate that fell. As the waiter got up from the floor and tried to help the man his wife started yelling at him loudly.

"Why is Sophia calling you here? She's only supposed to be your secretary! It's way after hours and she sure as hell shouldn't have your cell number!" The woman shouted, throwing the phone at him. "I knew something was going on between the two of you but you kept denying it! Well you can stay with her tonight, and you better take a cab because the car is mine!"

With that said the woman kicked back out of her chair, grabbed her purse and stormed out of the restaurant. The man just sat there stunned by everything that had gone wrong in just under two minutes.

"Wow that was intense." Daniel said, the excitement of making it happen hitting him like a caffeine rush.

"It always is." She smiled wickedly. "That was pretty lame though, but it was a start. I tweaked her emotions a little for dramatic effect. It works every time. Now imagine how their fight is going to affect the people around them. Any issues people have will be worse, and situations will become tense. It all works in our favor. It's really all quite a domino effect."

"It's amazing how things are. If he didn't have the phone out-"

"But he did, and everybody does. His wife's phone was inside her purse but easy to reach. It's the age of technology and attention getting. The human ego is bigger than Jesus these days." A wicked smile curled the sides of her lips up. "Everybody knows what everybody else is doing, and most people lie about themselves so much it's pathetic. Before long people will be bar coded and have electronic implants that will do everything for them so they don't even have to get out of bed in the morning."

"I guess they don't appreciate life for what it is." He thought about it for a second and then added, "But I guess that's what keeps us in business."

"You're absolutely right. If humans actually used their brains and their emotions at the same time we wouldn't even have a reason to be."

Daniel remembered that he had yet to replace what he'd taken out of Hell, and thought he'd get started by calling on some imps to get a few things from the restaurant patrons. Most of them seemed well to do, which was a good thing for him. A lost earring or ring, even a wallet or two wouldn't matter to them.

"I just sent out a few imps." Daniel informed her with a whisper.

"You called on them from here?" When Daniel nodded she smirked at him. "Good, you're really picking up on things. You realize of course that you're going to have to appoint someone new to take over for Dantalian? You can't just keep running things in his territory by yourself. If you do you run the risk of being challenged."

"I'll take care of it tonight." He felt the darkness rising up within him, like a second voice that knew what to say and do before he did. He dismissed it, thinking it was just the price of gaining experience.

Lilith's eyes widened as a waiter brought their dinner.

"Let's take a break and savor this duck, it looks excellent."

By the time they finished dinner it was late, but rather than take a cab Daniel brought them back to the bedroom of the hotel suite by using his shadow.

"Now I've got to get to that pit and straighten things out." Daniel said. "I'll see you soon." He took pleasure in a long kiss from Lilith, reluctant to be pulled away, then stepped into the darkness of his shadow and went to Hell.

"He certainly has potential." Lilith mumbled watching him vanish. "A good lover too, a little clumsy at first but everyone is. It's a shame what's going to happen to him."

There was a knock on the door.

Lilith froze, surprised, and then sensed who it was as she walked into the living room of the suite. *"What's he doing here?"* she wondered, swinging the door open.

"Christian?"

He fell into her arms, an exhausted foul smelling mess. His lips were crusted with the blood he'd been constantly coughing up along the way and his ankle finally gave out when he passed through the doorway. Lilith grabbed him before he fell. Christian moaned. The pain from his unhealed ribs was still severe and persistent.

"Let me get you over to the couch." She said, pulling him over to it and kicking the door shut. She got him reclining on his back, took off his baseball hat and held his face in her hands. "Who did this to you? How did it happen?"

"I was going back into foster care, looking to get a few more souls for you before I paid another church a visit, but then he showed up." His words were tired and quiet, his breathing labored.

"Who?" Anger flashed in her eyes.

"It was B'lial's son, Louis Darque." He said breathlessly.

ELEVEN

After sending Bruce off Louis told Tindilli to go home.

"I probably should." He agreed. "I might even be able to get a few hours sleep and save my wife a lot of aggravation just by coming home."

"Absolutely," Louis smacked him on the back. "There's no point in sticking around right now. I'll be in Hell trying to find my brother. Elizabeth will be here waiting and keeping an eye on things. If anything happens we'll call you as soon as we can."

"Alright," he said hesitantly. "I'll give you

a call in a few hours if I don't hear from you by then."

Louis stayed by the door, watching him drive off.

"I get the feeling this is going to be a rough night." Louis lit a cigarette and lightly closed the door.

"Did you say something?" Elizabeth asked, coming up behind him.

"No, it was nothing." He said dismissively. "How are you holding up during all this crazy stuff?"

"I'm okay," she said brightening. "I've gone through worse with you."

"I think I need another cup of coffee before I leave. I need a jolt of something." Louis walked with her back to the kitchen. "I hope you don't mind staying here while I'm gone. Just leave a window open for Bruce. I'm sure he'll type up a message if he finds anything."

Elizabeth sat down at the table and Louis poured himself coffee.

"Can I get you some?" He asked.

"No that's okay," she replied. "Now that we have a minute, can we talk?"

"I figured we'd do that sooner or later." He grinned at her and tapped his cigarette in the ashtray. "It's good to see you again."

"You too. I'm really sorry I let you think I was dead. I was just so afraid for you. I mean, I was there when B'lial pinned you to that tree like a butterfly in a display case." She stared off. "You'd been through so much, and unlike me, you never asked for any of it, it was all just thrown at you. I didn't think that was fair, you didn't deserve any of it, but there wasn't really much I could do about it."

"You did fine." He smiled at her. "You helped me when I really needed it, and you didn't have to. That means a lot. You really could have gotten killed going against B'lial the way you did. It was a very brave thing to do." He reached out and took her hand. "I appreciate you being there before and I do now."

"Do you think we can pick up where we left off?" She asked pensively.

"That's a little bit of a sticky subject right now." He smashed out his cigarette and looked her in the eyes. "Diane was able to come and see me a few days ago. She told me some things, and sort of gave me the 'okay' to live my life because no matter what, the love we shared would always survive."

"She's right. Your love, that part of you will always endure and return to her when the time comes." Her eyes saddened. "I'm so sorry you lost her."

"The way she explained it, being with you wouldn't be any threat to what we had, more like a separate part of me." He looked hopeful, but nervous. "So, maybe we can pick up from where we left off. I just think we'd need to take things a little slow. Life is pretty complicated these days."

"Okay, I can live with that." She said.

"I'd better get going." Louis finished his coffee and got up. "I really want to get this over with, and I don't want to fight him."

"Are you sure you don't want me to go with you? I could stay on the sidelines." Elizabeth asked. "He could come at you with a small army and you wouldn't even know it until it was too late."

"I know, I'm flying blind, but I'm going directly to Dantalian's pit, where he and I destroyed my father." He sighed, apprehensive. "I can find him from there no matter where he is because he's my brother. But I'll be prepared to jump through my shadow at the first sign of trouble. I've got to try to help him though, and if there's anything he knows about Christian or Lilith, I have to find out."

"Please just be careful, and if you need me you know I'm here." She stood up and kissed him on the cheek, his stubbly beard tickling her lips. Then she hugged him close as his shadow took shape alongside them.

"I'll be back soon." He passed her his house keys. "In case you need to leave for any reason. This neighborhood isn't what it used to be." Then he stepped through the darkness and into Hell.

****

Daniel reached Hell feeling uncharacteristically angry. He didn't understand where the anger came from, since he was actually in a pleasant mood only seconds ago when he was with Lilith.

"I should have done this already. I can't show weakness like this again, ever." He muttered aloud in Dantalian's pit. "I'll take care of it now, and no one will dare challenge me." He wanted to change into his demon form, but was reluctant to let go of his new face and body. It felt too good to be 'normal'.

He was about to call on the higher ranks of his minions to choose Dantalian's successor when suddenly he could sense that someone was there with him. It wasn't just someone, it was his brother.

Louis had just arrived, appearing in a small alcove. His shadow remained on the wall upon his command, and he stepped out into the open. Immediately he knew that Obscure was there, he could feel it.

"Hey, Obscure!" He called out, walking further into the open. "I know you're here. I'm just here to talk."

"I no longer answer to that name. I have another, and though I'd had it my entire life I never saw fit to use until now."

Louis heard his brother's words echo

around him. He followed the sound of his voice and saw him standing next to a rock formation, shrouded in shadows. The brother he knew as 'Obscure' stepped out of the shadows and revealed himself.

"I was Christened 'Daniel Smith' by a group of nuns at a convent that also served as a home for unwanted children and unwed mothers." He smiled at Louis, his suit crisp and new, dark hair was cut short and slicked back. His clean shaven features reminded Louis of himself but there were subtle differences too.

"Oh my god, this is incredible!" Louis said, recognizing his brother as a human, a regular person, but utterly shocked. "You look great! How is it you were able to do this? You never could before."

"With the darkness of my father I am whole, as I should have been at birth." He glanced at Louis looking annoyed. "Unlike you, I didn't have the advantage of being thought of as a normal person while growing up. I was either discarded or thought of as a monster because of how I looked."

"Uh oh, sounds like he's got a big ax to grind and he's looking for a scapegoat. I've got to tread lightly or this can turn into a shit-fest." Louis thought to himself.

"Why are you even here? You've no place in Hell, no reason to be here, and I thought I made it clear that you're not welcome here when I tossed you and your filthy little familiar out." Daniel walked closer to him, eyes piercing and red. "You've always led the privileged life. You didn't even know who your father was until a short time ago. I on the other hand, had to live with the curse of knowing him. The only reason I didn't kill myself was because I wanted something more. I wanted a normal life and I wouldn't give up or give him the satisfaction of knowing he drove me to suicide. Now I've got my chance to have everything I've ever wanted, ever dreamed of."

Daniel felt rage building inside him, but it was strange to him because he felt as if he were watching himself go through the motions of what he was doing and not actually doing it himself. His words sounded as if they came from someone else.

"Daniel, if that's what you prefer to be called," Louis said, standing his ground as his brother drew closer. "I didn't even know you existed when I was growing up. What happened isn't my fault anymore than it's yours. I thought we'd both established that when we destroyed B'lial together. If I'd known you were alive all those years ago I would have done everything I could to have made sure you had a good life, that we were brothers in more than blood and genetics."

Daniel's expression softened, his eyes returned to normal. In the back of his mind he still felt the rage, but he held it back, wouldn't allow it to control him.

"I came here to talk to you, not to argue or fight." Louis implored. "There's something going on in the city, murders being committed. I won't go into detail unless you want me to, but everything that's happening, it all looks tied to B'lial, like he's either behind it or someone is doing it for him."

"How can that be?" Daniel felt confused. "We defeated him soundly, and I tore his heart out myself, taking from it what I needed." He thought, *"B'lial is gone, I'm whole because we destroyed him. He can't come back, I won't let him!"*

"Well, there are a lot of reasons, but one of the big ones is, demons don't really die." Louis kept his voice even, calm, not wanting to get Daniel angry, so they could speak on good terms. "I think he's trying to come back, trying to 'buy' his way back with souls. There's a young boy out there, the son of Lilith. He's killing people, collecting souls for his mother. I think she's going to use them to bring B'lial back."

Daniel's eyes widened at what Louis had said. His words made sense, but he couldn't fully grasp them because anger got in the way. It wasn't just anger, it was rage, and even though he didn't want to feel it, the emotion was taking control of him.

"You're out of your mind if you think I'm going to believe that. I know her! I know Lilith!" Daniel, eyes glowing again, felt himself involuntarily beginning to change into his demon form. He was caught by surprise since he hadn't brought on the change himself, and stopped the transformation. Instead, he swung at Louis as hard as he could.

Louis saw the punch coming and ducked below it. As Daniel pulled his arm back he shoved him powerfully with both hands into the formation of rocks behind him.

"It doesn't have to be like this! I told you I'm not here to fight!" Louis growled, eyes glowing as red as Daniel's. "If you want to turn this into a brawl it's not going to happen! Personally, I didn't think that having B'lial's darkness inside you was affecting you, but now that I see how you're acting I think it is, and not in a good way. I also think Lilith is using you to bring B'lial back."

Daniel felt like he'd snapped out of a trance when he slammed into the rocks. His mind still felt a little clouded. What Louis said made him angry, but it was different then the senseless rage he'd felt only a moment ago.

"What you're saying can't be true!" He shouted, walking back to face Louis again. "You're just jealous that I have a life now and a good one too! You can't take that away from me!"

"I don't want to take anything from you! Prove me wrong Daniel! Just prove me wrong! Honestly, I'd like to be wrong just because I want you to have everything you missed out on. I resent what B'lial did to you, and I wish things were different between us too, but there's nothing I can do to change any of that. All I can do now is hope I'm wrong about everything I told you tonight."

"I'll prove it." Daniel said, determined to do just that. "I don't know anything about a boy, but I can bring Lilith here. She'll tell you herself how fuckin' crazy what you're saying is!"

"No, I want to meet on earth." Louis said sternly. He didn't want to walk into a trap or get torn apart by an army of Daniel's minions either. "There's an abandoned warehouse on 8th and 46th, meet me there at midnight tonight." He looked at Daniel sympathetically. "Daniel, I really hope I'm wrong, especially about B'lial's darkness."

Without saying another word, Louis turned and stepped through his shadow in the alcove, walking out of it in the center of his kitchen.

Daniel wanted to howl out his anger, wanted to break something, hurt someone, but he couldn't even tell why. Was it Louis and what he said about Lilith? *"No, Lilith couldn't be using me to help bring B'lial back. She wouldn't do that to me, not after all we've shared."* He said with certainty.

****

"He's very powerful." Christian said breathlessly. "I don't think I've ever been hit that hard before. I hurt so much I couldn't even focus enough to cast an illusion. I had to hide in the shadows and steal clothes to get here."

"Louis Darque is a son of B'lial, he's going to be very powerful. So, do you think he's on to us?" Lilith asked Christian. She had her hand pressed against his broken ribs in order for them to mend more quickly.

"He knows I'm killing people for a reason," he said, feeling stronger already, "but I don't think he knows what the reason is. I guess if he did he wouldn't have been looking for me, he'd have been looking for you instead."

"And that bitch is still alive too." Her words trailed off, then she added under her breath, "I knew she wasn't dead, I just knew it. B'lial builds them stronger than that. I'll have to take care of her myself."

"Where does this leave us now?" Christian asked. "Do we still have a lot of souls left to pass on?"

"No, we're just about there, just a few

more." She lifted her hand off his side and pinched his cheek with a grin. "You should be fine in a little while, son. The ribs are back where they belong and they're nearly healed. Now aren't you glad I'm around to help you out?"

Christian nodded painfully. His head hurt every time he moved it, even lying down.

"Now you've got to go. I know you're still in rough shape but at least you can move around more freely now." Lilith went over to the bar and made herself a drink. "You really shouldn't be here anyway. He could return anytime and he doesn't know any of my 'children' are around."

"So the other brother is here, with you?" He asked, sounding confused.

"Of course." She grinned.

"But I thought his days were num-"

"Shhhh, don't talk about it." Lilith said cutting her son off. "Now just be a good little boy and get out of here."

Christian sat up. He pressed down on his ribs and took a deep breath. Satisfied that he no longer felt any pain there, he swung his legs down from the couch and tested his ankle. It was still sore but he could put his weight on it and more than likely walk on it for at least a while before having to rest again.

"Too late, he'll be here in a few seconds." Lilith looked over at him. "I can mask your presence from him but you still need to hide. I suggest under the bed, hurry!" She urged him.

Christian ran into the bedroom, dropped to the floor and slid under the bed as quickly as he could. He heard Daniels' footsteps coming from the living room a split second later.

"Lilith, I need to speak to you." Daniel growled, stepping out of his shadow.

"How did things go? Were you able to find a suitable successor?" Lilith asked innocently.

"No, I didn't even look yet. I've got something a little more important to contend with right now." He slumped down on the couch. "My brother showed up when I was there and we had a little discussion."

"Oh?" She said, trying not to sound concerned, even though she was. "I hope it wasn't anything too serious. It doesn't look as if you've been in a fight."

"It was very serious. I need to ask you a few things." His eyes narrowed at her. "Can you sit with me for a moment please?"

"Certainly." She dropped down beside him on the couch and stroked his cheek with her fingers. "You look upset. Why don't we go out for a late lunch and talk things over somewhere relaxing."

"I'd really rather get this out in the open and then if things are okay then maybe we can still go out. My brother Louis brought a few things to my attention." Daniel felt the rage building up inside him again, and was frustrated because it was as if the emotion recently had a mind of its own. He wasn't angry at Lilith, he just wanted some answers. "Are you doing something to resurrect my father? Do you have a son that's nearby killing people for you?"

"That bastard Louis did figure things out." Lilith thought to herself angrily. *"I bet that bitch Elizabeth is helping him too! Wait'll I get my hands on her!"*

"I don't understand. What do you mean 'resurrect B'lial'." She replied, trying to sound as casual and innocent as possible. "And as for children, I've had countless children over the centuries. Keeping track of just one would be rather difficult, if not impossible."

"I need to know if you're somehow working on bringing my father back, getting B'lial resurrected. I know that may sound crazy to you, but I need you to answer honestly." Daniel leaned back in the couch and stared at her. "My brother and I are going to meet tonight at midnight. You have to come along with me. I need to prove to him that he's wrong. I need to show him that you're not helping anyone bring our father back. I'd like to hear it from you first, unless of course he's right."

"I'm not doing anything for anybody these

days except you." She smiled at him, then held his face in her hands and kissed him on the mouth. *"I guess technically I'm not really lying."* She thought to herself. *"After all, B'lial is inside him."*

TWELVE

Louis stepped out of his shadow, into the kitchen of his brownstone and immediately his sense of smell was assaulted with the powerful aroma of breakfast. The kitchen smelled as if he had stepped into a diner. He looked at the old gas stove that sat apart from the counter across the room and laughed.

"That's got to be the best work-out you've had in ages." He laughingly said to the stove, noting that there was still a frying pan sitting on an unlit burner. The scent of bacon grease coming from it was wonderfully intense. In a quick move he let his overcoat slide off his arms, caught it before it hit the floor and flung it onto a hook by the kitchen door.

"Do you always talk to your appliances?" Elizabeth came up behind him with a hug.

"Why not, I talk to a raven on a daily basis." He replied dryly. "I never said I was sane."

"I hope you don't mind, I went out and took the liberty of grocery shopping for you both." She took the frying pan off the stove and put it in the sink, running hot water in it and leaving it to soak. "Bruce was right, you were out of everything. I don't know how you live the way you do."

"Shopping used to be fun, but lately it's the lowest thing on my list of priorities." He lit a cigarette and dropped into a kitchen chair. "Cooking has been a little tough too. I used to love to do it before, but now-"

"Well, I made eggs, bacon, some pancakes, just the basics, nothing fancy." Her expression brightened. "I haven't cooked in a long time either so it was a fun diversion. I just finished before you got here. It's all covered up and waiting on the counter."

"Wow! You might just have to move in." He joked, seeing how much she'd made.

"I'm glad you're back safe. I don't see any wounds either, so I guess you didn't get in a fight." She looked him up and down. "So how'd it go otherwise?"

"I'm not even sure where to start," Louis rubbed his eyes and put his head back. "Did Bruce get back yet?"

"I'm afraid not." Elizabeth leaned back against the counter and looked at the open window. "I keep looking over there hoping he'll pop in the window with good news. That was another good reason to get out for a few minutes, cooking too, it kept me occupied. I'm not good with waiting, never have been."

"I hope he gets here soon, the sooner the better." Louis sighed. "I worry a lot about the little guy, he's like family now."

"Tell me what happened with your brother." She pulled the chair across from him out and sat down. "Did you get a lead on Christian?"

"My brother is so different now, not that I knew him well to begin with. He just seemed distant, angry one second and happy the next; almost confused. I imagine that's from having that piece of B'lial inside him like you warned me about. I didn't even want to explain that to him too much because it would have definitely started a fight. He did admit that he knows Lilith, but not Christian. According to him, Lilith's a real sweetheart. I can only guess, but with her being who she is, I get the feeling they're involved, as in being a 'couple'." Louis laughed dryly. "Isn't that great? I think my brother is screwing around with the first woman ever created, and she's evil incarnate."

"It figures, and for us, that's really not a good thing. Lilith is the mother of manipulation." She said. "She knows more about sin then anyone short of God and the Master."

"Did I mention my brother's new name and 'look'?" Louis said half-heartedly. "He can change his appearance now and look like a normal person. He sort of looks like me, only clean shaven and without a cleft in his chin. I guess the resemblance is normal in fraternal twins, but it still freaked me out a little. He goes by the name 'Daniel Smith' now too. He said it was given to him by the nuns that found him as a baby. I didn't even know nuns found him."

"How much do you actually know about him?" Elizabeth asked.

"Not a whole hell of a lot. Only the things he told me about himself and his life, and none of it was nice. I feel terrible about it because his life was horrible, and in spite of everything happening now, mine wasn't. I can't even imagine how he had to have been living all these years. I can understand why it's such a big deal to look normal, to be able to walk around and be accepted. Again, I'm guessing here, but if he looked the way he looked when I met him, stuck in a demonic form, and he was that way all his life, then I seriously doubt he's ever had sex. That would make Lilith his first, that is, if they've actually done the dirty deed."

"Knowing her and her reputation, they have in every way possible. He's probably in love with her, and if she's got his claws in him he'll do anything she asks." Elizabeth shook her head.

"I confronted him with the idea that she's using him. He denied it of course, but wanted to prove she wasn't. I got him to agree to meet me at midnight over at the warehouse we were just at. It's big and empty, so if it comes down to a fight we'll have room to move and we won't be in plain sight. If only I could get him to ditch B'lial's darkness. If I could get him to rid himself of that, then he would be able to think with a clear head." Louis jumped when Bruce abruptly flew in through the window.

The raven paused momentarily to cackle at them, and then continued on, flying upstairs.

"He must have a lot to tell us." Louis grinned and pointed in the direction that he flew in. "The typewriter's up there. I always keep a clean sheet of paper in it for him too."

Tense moments passed while they waited quietly for Bruce to come back downstairs. The sound of the keys on the typewriter tapping sounded overly loud.

The sound stopped and they could hear Bruce's wings flapping toward them. The raven flew to the kitchen table and hovered to drop the sheet of paper he held in his claws, then he landed next to it, nudging the paper in Louis' direction.

"Let's see what we've got here." He said, reading the paper.

FOUND
KID HURT
GO IN PARAMONT
SMELL EGGS
HUNGRY BAD
COFFEE

"Bruce you did great! Thanks for helping, and yes you can have some eggs." He looked at Elizabeth. "Here, read this." He handed her the paper. "He found Christian, and the spelling is off but I think Bruce means the Paramount Hotel. We're gonna have to make breakfast quick if we plan on getting to the Paramount to catch the kid but at least we have a little time. Christian is going to need some to heal so he won't be going anywhere for a little while at the very least. I wonder if he's staying with just Lilith or if my brother is involved too. I should have asked him where he's staying on earth."

As soon as Louis mentioned Lilith's name, Bruce nodded and squawked in agreement.

"Did you see her?" He asked.

Bruce nodded and then gestured with his whole body toward the covered plates on the counter. He was truly famished.

"You must be famished after flying around so much. I guess now is as good a time as any for breakfast." He nodded to Elizabeth. "She cooked for us, so you may want to thank her."

Bruce spun around and cackled at Elizabeth. He walking over to one of her hands, nudging it with his beak.

"Anytime Bruce, I don't mind. I'll even fix you up a plate with a little of everything on it." She said, getting up. "I'll just heat it all up in the microwave and we can dig in. Did you want to get in touch with Tindilli?"

"I'll let him sleep, he could use the rest. I'll give him a call and tell him what's going on before we leave for the hotel. That way we can get the kid, question him and still have time to meet my brother later."

"Are you going to let Tindilli come with us tonight?" She asked, heating the plate of eggs she made in the microwave. "It's going to be dangerous."

"Us?" Louis made a face at her.

"You weren't thinking of going alone were you?" Elizabeth looked annoyed. "They could be setting up a trap."

"I imagine they are, and you're right. If I tell Tindilli what's going on he'll come no matter how I tell him not to. As for you, well you saved my ass once already, I guess I don't mind if you come along to do it again."

Elizabeth bore a satisfied smile while dishing out breakfast.

****

Daniel slipped on his jacket, straightened his tie and then looked himself over in the mirror on the bedroom door. His face and body still amazed him. He laughed to himself when he realized he must have felt like a child on Christmas morning every time he looked in a mirror.

"Are you gonna be long?" He called out to Lilith.

"No I just left my lipstick in the bathroom," she said stepping out of the room and closing the door behind her. She absently tapped the side of the bed. "We'd better get a move on if we want to beat the afternoon crowd to that little restaurant I want to bring you to. Then there are some people I'd like you to meet."

"People?" Daniel's brow quirked up.

"Yes, trust me, it'll be fun." She flashed him a smile. "It's a beautiful day outside too. We can take our time and walk to the restaurant." She put her arm around him.

"Yeah, that sounds nice." Daniel smiled at her, furious that Louis could even think she was using him.

****

When he was sure they were long gone, Christian struggled to slide out from under the bed.

"It was much easier getting under here than it is getting out." He grumbled. His wounds weren't quite healed yet but he felt much better standing up since before he went into hiding. Remembering that Lilith was in the bathroom and mentioning lipstick gave him the silent cue to check the room out.

As he suspected, there was a note for him written in lipstick on the mirror from her.

"Stay in the suite until tomorrow"

"What?" He said aloud. "I want to be out and about and having fun! This is ridiculous!"

There was a knock at the door.

"Housekeeping!" A woman with a heavy Spanish accent called out from the hallway. She tapped the door again sounding impatient.

"Maybe I can still have a little fun and even get Lilith another soul while I do it." He stepped over to the door and looked through the peephole. The woman was short with long straight black hair. Her face was boney but her lips were full and her body thin, not his usual but he found it oddly attractive. Christian estimated that she couldn't be a day over thirty, and she felt 'dirty' to him when he delved into her mind, as if she had many sins to play with. "Ya gotta love a woman in uniform."

Christian shrugged out of his oversized sweatshirt and cast an illusion on himself that made him look like a young Ricardo Montalban.

"I think I'll drive her like a Chrysler Cordoba, with soft Corinthian leather, and then rip out her heart," he thought, smiling wickedly.

Christian opened the door and welcomed the woman in with open arms.

****

Bruce waited patiently on the ledge outside the hotel. Louis and Elizabeth had just gone inside. Still wired from sipping too much coffee, he shifted his weight from one foot to another, remembering the plan Louis had come up with at the brownstone, hoping everything would work out.

"All we have to do is find out what room Lilith is in." Louis said.

"What if she didn't use her real name? Or maybe she's staying with someone else?" Elizabeth pointed out.

"Well, if that's the case we can always just try to pick up on her or Christian. I can sense their evil and I'm sure you can too. We can home in on it and find out that way."

"We'd have to walk each floor!" Elizabeth glared at him. "Do you realize how large that hotel is?"

"So? We have time if we have to. Don't worry, we'll find him one way or another. We'd still have the element of surprise." Louis said dismissively.

Elizabeth nodded, but Bruce could tell she was a little frustrated.

"I'd drive us to the hotel, but my damn car hasn't shown up yet. The tow truck should have been here with it already, but I guess since I paid by credit card over the phone he's taking his time." He stood up and grabbed his coat. "We'd better get going. I know an ally nearby where we can show up without being seen."

So they left Bruce outside and walked into the hotel trying to look as casual as possible. The lobby was practically empty. The clerk, an older man, had just handed a keycard to a young couple that had just checked in.

"Hi, I'm sorry to bother you, but I'm working with the local PD and I was wondering if you could give me some information. I need a listing of all the guests that checked in over the past week." Louis asked, flashing his identification.

"Sir, we don't usually do that sort of thing." The man said, taken aback and slightly nervous. "Our guests like their privacy."

"If you'd like I could call the detective I'm working with on this particular case and he could ask you for it himself. I'm sure he could also get a warrant within the hour if he had to." Louis put his wallet away, brow forming a straight line over his eyes.

"Louis, let me speak to him." Elizabeth

winked at him.

"Ma'am, I'm sorry but-" A visible sheen of sweat had formed on the man's forehead.

"But you really just wanted to help us out, so our trip here wouldn't have been a waste of time, right?" Elizabeth cut him off and stared at him intently. "We can really use a master keycard as well, since we may have to search the room if no one is there."

The man's expression changed and he smiled at her.

"Why sure, ma'am, I'll print you a list and get you a card. I just need a second." He pulled up the information on his flat screen below the counter and then the small inkjet on a desk behind him began to print the list. He gathered the papers and a keycard and handed it to Elizabeth.

Louis stood next to her, flabbergasted.

"What the hell was that? I didn't know you could do that." Louis said in a hushed whisper, slightly annoyed. "Why didn't you just do that to begin with?"

"You're always so confident, it was nice to see you try and fail." She gave him a wicked grin and walked over to one of the couches to sit down.

Louis followed her. She handed him one of the papers and they both looked them over for Lilith's name.

"Is there any other name that she's been

known to go by?" He asked.

"From what I know she seems compelled to go by her real name, but her last name would vary. So anyone named Lilith would do. It's not a very common name anyway." She replied, her eyes running down each line on the paper.

"Never mind Lilith," Louis whispered. "My brother is here." He held out the paper to her and pointed to his name. "It's him. Daniel Smith checked in 3 days ago."

****

"My name is Lilith, and I'm an addict." Lilith had a look of mock sadness on her face.

"Hi Lilith," the men and women sitting in a small circle of chairs around them said in unison. Some of them held large coffee cups from a local deli two doors down.

"I'm an addict and I love it. I know all of you have your vice; that's why you're here, but are they really vices?" She turned to look at Daniel, who sat next to her. "I don't think they are, do you Daniel."

"No," he replied flatly.

"I always thought everything I did was fun, and people were just so jealous of it that they wanted me to stop." Lilith's eyes bore into each person there, fishing for their sins, their vices. She fed on their misery, their memories and pain. It was like a drug to her, and she craved more.

Some of the people were strong, too strong for her to manipulate easily. They were the first ones in the circle to start shaking their heads. One by one they simply got up and left, while the few that remained looked as if they were deep in thought; staring off, trans-like.

"You for instance, Tanya," Lilith pointed to a young woman. "You like to smoke, and I don't mean cigarettes. It made you feel good right?" The girl nodded vigorously, and Lilith continued on, "Well, there's a bathroom right here. I bet if you go in there right now, you'll find exactly what you need to enjoy yourself. You can do your thing with no one the wiser. I'm sure nobody here would interfere with you. Certainly not Joe over there," she pointed to an older man seated across from her. "He's going to be making some calls, placing some bets, and he might even have a drink or two later on, right Joe?"

The old man looked shaken, but then a look of determination formed in his expression and he nodded. "Yes, I think I'll do just that. It's been too long since I had some real fun."

Daniel watched each one of the remaining people give in to their own dark needs and desires. He couldn't explain why, since he'd never felt that way before, but their pain was invigorating for him.

"I feel strong Lilith," he said gruffly.

"You're half demon, it's natural for the

pain of others to bring you pleasure. Enjoy it. It will help give you the energy you need to face your brother tonight."

By the time he and Lilith left the basement of the local library, Tanya was unconscious on the bathroom floor only minutes away from aspirating on her own vomit. Joe had lost most of what he had left in his retirement account and several others were either having sex on the tables or in the far corner of the room, cutting themselves with any sharp object they could find.

"I feel it." Daniel said wistfully, as they left the library.

"Wait until you read about it in the paper tomorrow. It might even make the morning newscast." Lilith smiled at him. "These people strengthen us by broadcasting the misery to the masses where it can be worshipped more than their own god."

She felt Tanya finally die in the bathroom. Then the wicked soul that Christian had just dispatched from Daniel's hotel suite added to the already long list of those fallen to raise B'lial.

"We only need one more, and I know the perfect victim, she thought to herself, *"that bitch Elizabeth! Louis is sure to bring her with him and destroying her will bring back B'lial, and put the last nail in Louis Darque's coffin!"*

THIRTEEN

When they got to the room, Elizabeth swiped the keycard in the door. When the green light flicked on Louis carefully opened the door. He stuck his head inside the living room of the suite and saw that it was clear.

"Let's go," he whispered in her ear.

The living room was empty. There was a glass door leading to a small balcony with a patio set on it, but no one was visible outside. The only other door they saw was across the room. Louis stepped over to it with Elizabeth on his heels. He counted down on his fingers and then flung open the door, making his way inside the bedroom.

There was a massive king size bed in the center of the room, Christian was lying on it, apparently from what they saw, sleeping.

"What the fuck are you doing here?" He said jumping up in bed. His mouth and chin were covered in dried blood, as were his hands.

Almost immediately Christian began the transformation into his demon form, but Louis rushed forward and backhanded him across the face, knocking him back down on the bed again.

"Don't even try it!" Louis shouted. He grabbed Christian by the throat and lifted him in the air, his eyes glaring red at the boy. "I went easy on you before and I still beat you, so just imagine what it'll be like if you really piss me off!"

Christian went limp, hoping to find an avenue of escape somehow after Louis released him.

"I'm going to put you down now, but if you try to move or get away, you're done." Louis threatened.

"Louis, we've got a little problem here." Elizabeth called out from the bathroom.

"Get up," he growled at Christian. "Show me what she's talking about."

Christian walked slowly into the bathroom, Louis right behind him. He could sense the rage in Louis, and for the first time in ages the boy knew fear.

Elizabeth stood in front of the shower stall shaking her head. Her hand clenched over her mouth and nose, her other hand pointed to the stall.

"Get in there," Louis roughly shoved Christian further into the room so that he nearly bumped into Elizabeth.

When Louis got to the shower stall, he wanted to scream and tear Christian limb from limb because of what he'd done. There was a naked woman hanging from the showerhead a leather belt secured tightly around her neck. Her eyes had been torn out, her throat ripped open, and there was a large hole where her heart used to be. There was little blood, but a lot of bite marks and torn flesh. The smell in the room was horrendous; adding to the rage Louis felt building inside him.

"She was a real whore." Christian stammered. "You wouldn't believe how many guests she's screwed, and for a married woman too-"

"You miserable bastard!" Louis twisted away from the shower stall and wrapped his hand around Christian's throat, lifting him from the ground and slamming him into the mirror above the vanity, shattering the glass and cracking the wall behind in. Christian struggled to get free, legs kicking at the sink and vanity, hands clenching frantically at Louis, but again he was much too strong.

"Louis!" Elizabeth shouted, grabbing his other arm. "Put him down!"

"I'll put him down alright, like a fucking rabid animal I'll put him down!" Louis eyes changed color, flashing to red, and his body started to change.

"Calm down!" Elizabeth grabbed his chin and turned his face toward her. "Remember what we have to do!" She pleaded.

"He's got to answer for this! Somehow he's got to answer for this!" Louis declared.

He took a deep breath and relaxed his body, still human. Slowly, with a look of death on his face as he stared at Christian, he pulled him back away from the wall. The boy stood on his own two feet, body shuddering in pain.

"We'll work something out, he'll pay for what he's done, but your brother needs to see him, to know what's really going on tonight." Elizabeth said.

"I need to get Tindilli here, he's got to get this mess cleaned up, notify her family." Louis' words were an angry hiss. "Then I want to talk to you! And I want answers!" He pulled Christian's face right up to his own. "Hold onto this piece of shit while I make the call."

He thrust Christian roughly at Elizabeth and walked away, out of the bathroom. The quick press of a button connected him to Tindilli.

"Hey, good to hear from you." Tindilli chuckled. Louis could tell he was gnawing on a cigar. "I was actually on my way to your house."

"Well, you better beeline it to the Paramount Hotel." Louis sighed in the phone. "We found the kid, Christian, but we found a body here with him too. I guess he needed a little snack. It's not pretty."

"Should I send out for a team?" He sounded harried.

"Maybe you should have a look at things first. I'm gonna question the little bastard right now to see what I can get out of him." Louis walked outside to the patio, lit a cigarette and sat down at the glass table.

"Let's get this over with!" Elizabeth dragged Christian outside with her, flinging him over to the table by Louis.

"Don't even think about trying to escape. I can change with the blink of an eye and tear you to shreds." Louis growled.

Ribs injured yet again, every breath felt like fire in his chest. Christian couldn't even concentrate hard enough to change anymore or even cast an illusion. He silently hated being stuck at the age he was, and wished he could have used the souls he'd recently acquired to age more rather than pass them onto his mother.

"I want to know what your mother is up to!" Louis pounded a fist on the table. "Is she trying to bring back my father? Is she bringing back B'lial?"

"You already know the answer to that." Christian said gravely, coughing up blood. "It's only a matter of time."

"Why?" He demanded. "Why would she want to bring him back?"

"She has to. She owes him for helping her when she was banished." Christian wiped the blood off his mouth with his sleeve and tried to breath slowly so he wouldn't cough again.

Elizabeth, who had stood with her back to both of them, finally turned around. She pointed at Christian angrily.

"You didn't have to kill anyone for her. You did that on your own." She shouted at him.

"I needed to feed on something, anything and the woman was there." He hung his head and held back a coughing fit that rattled his ribs anyway. "It's what I do. It's what I was created to do. I couldn't stop myself if I wanted to."

"When does Lilith plan on resurrecting B'lial?" Louis asked. He heard someone knock on the door and knew it had to be Tindilli. "Elizabeth, can you let Tindilli in?"

She nodded and went back inside.

"Was my brother aware of you being a part of this? Did he know you and your mother were trying to bring B'lial back?" He asked.

Christian didn't respond. Louis stood up and punched him the head.

"I asked you a question, I expect an answer." Louis cracked his knuckles and gritted his teeth. "Don't make this get any uglier than it already is."

"I'll answer you, but understand this. I may be this age, looking like a kid, but you know what I am." He lifted his head to stare directly at Louis. "I like what I am. I enjoy feeling the life slip away from my prey. You, you're just a wannabe human being masking yourself with empathy, which is just petty and foolish."

Louis pulled his fist back, then stopped himself in mid-swing.

"I won't let him get under my skin anymore than he already has."

"Just answer the question you little shit." He spat.

"No, your brother, Obscure, or 'Daniel', what he likes to call himself now, has no idea I'm even here." Christian hung his head again.

"Well, you probably already know about the meeting we're having in a couple of hours. The surprise is, you're coming with us, and you're going to tell him exactly what you just told me."

"Louis?" Elizabeth said, poking her head outside. "Tindilli needs you inside. Go ahead; I'll keep an eye our guest."

He took one last drag from his cigarette and then stepped on it walking back into the living room of the suite. He found Tindilli in the bathroom wearing rubber gloves, checking on the crime scene.

"Here, put these on." He handed Louis a pair of gloves. "This is one nasty homicide. I've got to call it in, there's no way we can clean this up and keep it quiet. The woman has a wedding ring on, her family has to be notified."

"Okay, then I guess you have to call it in, there's nothing else we can do." Louis sighed, feeling defeated.

"There's more to it than that." Tindilli put his hand on Louis' shoulder. "How are we going to explain any of this? I mean, you've got the perp outside, but I'm guessing you're not going to let me take him in for any of the murders he's committed, right?"

"No, I can't. We need him right now. Believe me, I want him to answer for what he's done, but not now. He's going to be the living proof to my brother that Lilith is using him and trying to bring back B'lial." He looked at the body hanging in the shower stall and cursed to himself.

"We can't go on like this. Too much is going on without any explanations. We can't have these cases going cold." Tindilli said pulling out a cigar. "Well, aren't you going to introduce me?" he said, heading outside without waiting for Louis.

"This is Christian, I don't even know if he has a last name."

Louis said as he followed him outside.

"I've had quite a few last names," the boy mumbled.

"So you're the kid that did that?" Tindilli pointed toward the bathroom, holding back his anger. "I can't wait until we can take your life."

"Here's a little more pain to prevent you from getting any bright ideas about escaping." Louis punched Christian in the face again, then gave him a flat fist where he knew the kids' ribs were already broken. He knew Christian would heal quickly from the injuries, but the pain would indeed prevent him from attempting to escape, and allow him the certainty that he wouldn't need to turn into his demon form again.

Tindilli turned away from Christian when Louis swung at him and lit his cigar. The cell phone, as tiny as it was, felt huge in his jacket pocket. Tindilli walked to the railing on the patio and took in the view to calm himself before making the call to the precinct.

****

Lilith and Daniel were already walking to the warehouse. It was early so they took their time, window shopping and laughing about the people they saw walking the streets late at night.

"Are you sure you actually want to meet with your brother?" Lilith asked playfully. "You could always just send a legion of demons to take care of him for you. You don't need to get your hands dirty in any of this."

He stopped abruptly, his eyes staring intently at Lilith.

"I told him I would meet him and prove him wrong. That's what I'm going to do." He looked straight ahead again and continued walking. "There's no honor in tricking him."

"Honor? That's a word, a belief, that's not in our world." She snickered.

"I have to do this my way. He needs to know things aren't the way he thinks they are." Daniel said sternly.

"Oh, I understand now." She smiled at him. "That's pride."

"I guess it is," He laughed.

"Why don't we have some fun before we meet with your brother?" Lilith asked, spinning around and walking backwards to face him. "Let's find an old car, steal it, drive it somewhere and fuck around like crazy."

"Why an old car? Shouldn't we at least

break into something exotic?" He gave her a strange look. "We can find a parking garage and get a sports car or a limo."

"You're right, but a person with an expensive car isn't affected as much if it's stolen. It might be annoying, but they can replace it easily." She twirled around in front of him giggling. "An old cheap car has history, and it's needed. It means something to whoever owns it. When it's gone, stolen, it causes problems. Problems bring frustrations, bickering, you know what I mean. All the bad shit it would cause is good for us."

"Okay, if you insist." He grabbed her and kissed her hungrily. "Let's find ourselves a big old boat of a car and have some fun! Then we can go see my brother and prove to him that's he's just a fool."

FOURTEEN

It seeped up slowly from the street.

Droplets of thick liquid blackness, resembling hot tar spilled together then swirled upward, forming a shadowy whirling mass. Elizabeth stepped out of it first, dressed in a black bodysuit with boots up to her knees, her wavy dark hair pulled back into a ponytail. She pulled John Tindilli out with her. He looked around nervously, service revolver out, pointed low to the ground.

"The street's clear." Tindilli muttered.

Louis was the last one to stride out of the darkness, his shadow, which had been strained beyond its normal limits to get them there. Slung over his shoulder, a bit battered, with his arms and legs bound in thick chains, was Christian.

"Wow," Louis said, winded. "That was tough. For a minute there I had my doubts about all of us getting here in one piece." He put his hand on Elizabeth's shoulder. "Remind me never to transport four people like that again."

"Are you okay?" She asked.

"Yeah, just a little winded." He shrugged in spite of the weight of Christian on one of his shoulders.

They all looked up when they heard Bruce arrive. He cackled at them and flew off to circle the building.

"We should have just driven up in Tindilli's car." She replied dismissively.

"If this was a trap we'd have lost the element of surprise." Louis whispered. "I can sense my brother inside. There's someone else too, so I guess Lilith did come with him."

"She's in for a surprise." Elizabeth looked at Christian and shook her head. "I've got him masked for now, but I don't think I can hide him from her for more than a few minutes."

"I just need five or ten minutes at the most." He looked around, his senses fanning out. When he was certain there was nothing out of the ordinary he turned to nod at both

Elizabeth and Tindilli.

The streetlights in front of the warehouse were blown out, but there were several on the side road that still worked, illuminating that side of the building, shining through the high row of randomly broken windows.

"Let's go." Louis walked at a fast pace from the street to the entrance of the warehouse. He put Christian down against the wall only a few feet away from the entrance. "Keep your gun on him at all times, and if we're not out of there in ten minutes bring him in. I'll take him from there."

"Not a problem. Just be careful in there." Tindilli said nervously.

"He'll be fine, I've got his back." Elizabeth grinned at him.

Louis turned and headed for the door. She was right behind him.

"Ah, the prodigal son has arrived." Daniel scoffed.

He and Lilith were leaning on an old steel table next to a heap of dented and rusting file cabinets about twenty yards away from them. Louis saw that Daniel was still dressed up in a suit and tie, but he could smell sex.

"Well, I guess I know for sure now if they're screwing around. I've got to get him away from her, get B'lial out of him somehow." Louis thought.

"I don't think we've been properly

introduced." Louis called out, walking toward them with Elizabeth at his side. "Who's your friend?"

"I'm sure you know who I am." Lilith glared at him. "That filthy little whore you're with must have told you all about me by now."

"That bitch!" Elizabeth whispered angrily.

"Let's not resort to name calling." Daniel said calmly. "We're here for a reason. Let's get it over with. Say what you have to say Louis, and the truth will come out."

Daniel gestured to Louis with his hands when they were only a few feet away from them, utterly confident.

"Are you going to admit what you're doing?" Louis asked Lilith. "Or should I say what you're trying to do? Tell him about how you owe B'lial a favor. Tell him how you met our wonderful father after getting thrown out of Eden!"

"I have no idea what you're talking about." Lilith said innocently.

"Oh give me a break! Do you honestly think I came here to listen to you lie." Louis' eyes narrowed at Lilith, his anger building. He looked at his brother. "Daniel, she's been trying to resurrect B'lial, and if she succeeds we're no better off now than we were before. Everything we fought for in Hell will have been for nothing."

"He doesn't know what he's talking

about." Lilith retorted. "He's a fool that just wants to split us up. Your brother is jealous of you now that you have a life of your own, a life of happiness, pleasure."

"What she's saying certainly makes sense to me." Daniel agreed.

"Look Daniel," Louis said struggling for words. "I honestly didn't come here for an argument or to fight you. I'm not jealous of anything. I actually want you to be happy. I want you to have a life of your own. I hate what B'lial did to you, and how you've had to live up until this point."

"Then just leave." Daniel said calmly. "Walk away. Lilith said what she had to say. Leave us in peace."

"I can't do that if there's a chance B'lial could come back! Daniel, the darkness you took from him, I think it's messing with you, changing you and making you more like him. Can you get it out of your body?"

"Ah, there's what you wanted all along!" Daniel shouted. "You are jealous! Why else would you want me to turn back into what I was?" He clenched his hands into fists, eyes suddenly bulging with anger.

"No! That's not what I'm trying to do!" Louis couldn't get another word out before Daniel rushed at him, shoving him to the ground.

"Just get out of here! Don't make me

change. I don't want to fight you either!" Daniel growled, barely in control of the anger that called to him, bending his will and tempting him to change into his demonic form.

"You can't tell she's lying to you?" Louis shouted, furious. "Or is it the fact that you can't give up B'lial's darkness? Is it too powerful for you?" He got to his feet in time to watch Lilith go after Elizabeth. *"No! This can't be happening!"*

Daniel swung at him, hitting him full in the face when Louis couldn't take it anymore and let the change take over. He tore free of his human self, the flesh ripping and dangling from his limbs, his clothes a tattered mess. He saw the same thing happening to Daniel and cursed to himself for letting his dark side come out.

"Shadow!" he shouted, and dove through it when it appeared in front of him. A split second later the shadow appeared directly in front of Lilith just as she was about to reach Elizabeth. Louis stepped out and backhanded Lilith hard enough to send her flying backwards and into a pile of trash several yards away.

Louis twisted around just in time to see Daniel there. The two grappled, their wings pounding on their backs, sending them spinning into the air.

"Damn it Daniel! Stop this before it's too

late!" Louis yelled as the two spun around in midair.

"It's already too late!" His brother bellowed.

Just then Tindilli came into the warehouse, dragging Christian in behind him. Bruce flew in above them at the same time.

Daniel saw Tindilli come in, his eyes widened at the sight of the boy the man was bringing in with him. His body momentarily went limp, and Louis used that split second of weakness to his advantage, roughly flinging him away. By the time Daniel hit the floor Louis was soaring toward Christian. In a quick movement he grabbed the boy by the chains that bound his legs and lifted him into the air, spinning around to head back toward Daniel.

In the meantime Tindilli was running toward the scene, his gun pointed at Lilith as she climbed down from the pile of trash.

Elizabeth didn't know what to do first, but elected to go after Lilith, who was a clear threat to everyone there. She ran as hard and fast as she could, flipping into a kick when she was close enough, knocking Lilith back down again. Elizabeth landed in a forward roll immediately getting back on her feet again.

"Ask your girlfriend about him!" Louis yelled, tossing Christian at his brother.

Daniel caught the boy and just held him in the air, looking him over, dazed at the revelation that had just been handed him.

Louis landed a few feet away from him.

"I didn't want to have to do it this way." He said sadly. "I wanted her to admit what she was doing before her son was brought in. I didn't want you to have to find out this way."

Daniel still stood there, holding up Christian, shocked and angry.

"My entire life has been like this! It's always been one deception after another after another. The only peace I've ever known was living on the streets." His words were sullen. "Apparently life among the discarded and refuse was the only true living I've ever experienced!"

"Don't listen to him Daniel!" Lilith demanded. "He's lying to you!"

Christian twisted around in Daniels grasp, looking up at him, blood pounding in his ears from being upside for so long.

"Please, can you free me?" Christian asked timidly.

Daniel simply dropped the boy, staring at him with contempt.

"Tell me who you are boy!" he demanded. "Are you really a son of Lilith?"

Christian hesitated, seeing Lilith being confronted by Tindilli and Elizabeth. Bruce also backed them up by taunting her and trying to rake her with his claws.

Daniel grabbed Christian by the throat and

pulled him closer.

"Lilith," Daniel shouted resentfully. "Tell me, is this your son?"

Lilith stood there, trapped by Elizabeth, Bruce and Tindilli, unable to reach her son, unable to free him from the heavy looking chains and Daniel's powerful grip.

"Tell me! Has this boy been killing for you?" Daniel tightened his grip on Christian's throat and the boy made a gurgling sound.

"Free him and the three of us will destroy your brother and his bitch!" Lilith beckoned. "We can send that old cow they brought with them to Hell and feast on the agony in his soul! Then nothing can stop us!"

Louis approached his brother, angry that things had turned out the way they did, but hoping he could somehow turn things around.

"It doesn't have to be this way Daniel." He implored, flinching momentarily at the way Christian was struggling to breath, completely helpless. "We can fix this and move on from here. We just have to make sure that B'lial doesn't come back."

"Louis, I'm sorry," Daniel said calmly, "But this can't be fixed. My life has been a torturous mess. It's not your fault, not anymore than it is mine. The only person responsible for it isn't here. I don't want him to come back, not ever."

"Things don't have to stay this way." Lilith

beckoned again. "I've shown you what life can be like. You can have everything you've ever wanted, you're slightest desires, just free the boy and be with me!"

Daniel looked at her and then back at Louis.

"She thinks I'm a fool, to be toyed with." His eyes squinted angrily at Louis. "I know this is her spawn, her son, I can smell her stink on him."

Daniel pulled Christian closer so that the boy's back was against his chest. His hand still clutched the boy's throat.

Louis could only watch as the expression on his brother's face changed to one of rage, his eyes smoldering like hot coals as he brought his free hand up to rest on Christian's head, claws sinking painfully into his skull.

"God forgive me," Daniel said, realizing it was the first time he'd ever addressed God since he was a child and living in a church shelter.

"No!" Lilith shouted as loudly as she could, frantically trying to think of a way to get to her son.

Howling with fury and anguish, Daniels' arms worked as one and with a powerful movement he tore Christians head clean off of his body. For a moment he stood there motionless, Christians' head in one hand and his body in the other, blood spurting out of his throat, thick droplets covering both Daniel and Louis.

Louis felt like everything was moving in slow motion all of a sudden as he watched the scene unfold before him.

"Is this what you wanted when you used me!" Daniel shouted to Lilith who was screaming curses at him.

Abruptly, Daniel's eyes went wide and he let the head and body drop to the dirty floor.

His face contorted painfully and suddenly he was wracked with spasms. His body twisted and convulsed as he doubled over moaning.

Louis didn't realize what was happening until it was too late.

Daniel was changing yet again, bones bending and snapping as he grew even larger, skin stretching and tearing open. He shrieked in agony, falling to his knees, holding his head in his hands and then abruptly Daniel Smith, formerly known as Obscure, was gone, and in his place stood B'lial!

"I told you I'd be back for you, bastard!" The demon smiled at Louis.

Not The End

Nick Kisella is an author, editor, and semi-retired fitness professional. Primarily a horror author, he has also adapted several films into novels, most recently including 'The Mary Horror Trilogy', and 'I Spill Your Guts'. He's also penned several screenplays over the years. With over a dozen titles to his credit, his most recent works are comprised of the novel, 'Morningstars', 'The Beasts and the Walking Dead' and 'Lilith's Apple'. His latest novel, 'Darque & Onscure' is the much anticipated sequel to 'Morningstars'. Nick Kisella was born and raised in New Jersey but now resides in North Eastern Pennsylvania. A husband and father of twins, Nick prefers to write at night.

If you'd like to reach Nick Kisella you can contact him through his website: http://nickkisella.com/

Or if you prefer, on his Face Book page: https://www.facebook.com/nick.kisella

Nick Kisella

19293859R00116

Made in the USA
Middletown, DE
14 April 2015